Love, Sex & The Hustle

MAYA KEITH

ISBN: 0989171884
ISBN-13: 978-0989171885

DEDICATION

Sometimes you learn that great friends are made when you are older and have the ability to choose wisely. Thank you TJ, Diane, Nicole, Chastity, Amy, Lisa, Janette, Jessica and Dawn. To my mom Luisa, and my dad Juan, you've taught me never to settle. My husband Larry, you inspired some of this book., we will always be best friends. To my children Danny and Amary, you are my world.

QURON JACKSON

I heard the faint sound of the sirens as I knelt down to hold Jul as blood flowed from her head. Our lives would end on some real Bonny and Clyde shit and all I could think about is how my life of crime began..............................

My t-shirt stuck to my back with sweat as the hot and humid Brooklyn air hit. Maw, Qahira, Ali and I walked out of our building and headed up the street to the Laundromat. For as long as I could remember we've always lived in the same apartment building. Four of us kids lived with my grandmother. We call her "Maw". My brother Justice is the first born. Four years later came Qahira a year later I was born and nine months later came the baby Ali. Although we were all around the same age our personalities were all so different. Since Just was the oldest and we didn't have our father he had taken the role of our father making sure we had nice sneakers on and helping Maw with us. Qahira was our scholar she excelled in school and mothered all of us and tried her best to keep us at peace with one another. Me I was the jokester and the wild child there was nothing I wasn't scared of and lived life one day at a time. My brother Ali on the other hand was much different than we were real quiet and kept to himself he didn't have much of a personality.

1

I was turning 14 this year so I was going to be able to finally get a summer job. I was tired of being broke. The new Jordan's just came out and I was tired of wearing Just's sneakers. The ones he had gotten tired of them. This summer hand me downs was not an option. Not only would I be able to get a job but it was summer and the streets were calling me.

The summer brought hydrants, Coney Island and the girls in the short shorts. This summer was going to be live! There had already been two shootings this week and summer didn't officially start for another week.

I slowly walked behind my family trying to avoid being in that hot ass Laundromat. I looked up the block and saw Loc and Suko sitting on a gate next to the corner store. I hoped Maw hadn't seen them so she would let me back on the block. What was I thinking? She was like a hawk and already spotted them long before I did. Maw slowed her pace forcing me to catch up!

"How you doing Ms. Jackson," they both said in unison. "Hello boys, yah staying out of trouble." "Yes Mam!" She turned around and gave me the eye like I knew better. She didn't rock with Loc or Suko. We had all been friends since Kindergarten. Maw didn't like that Suko was usually my co-defendant when I was in trouble or kicked out of school. Loc's reputation was no better. He'd been in and out of juvi. I first met Loc in the building. He lived 2 floors up from me with his uncle. Suko's mother and Maw went to church together and that's how we got close.

"What up yah! I thought yah was going to wait on a brother." "You know how Loc get when it's too hot, plus we all know you aint going nowhere on laundry day." "You cracking Suko? Just cause you aint got no clothes to wash don't hate on me." We all laughed. We cracked jokes in front of the Laundromat for a minute until Maw had Ali come and get me to help fill the washers.

Maw was bugging having us do this while everyone was getting wet with the hydrants. It was the summer and this heat could knock a nigga out. "Maw, why Just aint washing his own ssssh stuff?" She looked up waiting for me to slip up and cuss. "Cause your brother is at his summer job." I looked at Qahira and smirked. Summer job? Please. We all knew he was on the block.

I was growing restless staring out the cloudy glass window inside the Laundromat. I was dying to hang out with my friends and seeing what trouble we could get into. Qahira was reading a book as usual. I watched her expressions as her glazed look told me she was no longer in Brooklyn and for that moment had become the character. Ali and Maw were watching the stories. "Ali come here real quick," he walked over like I had disturbed him from watching Young and the Restless. "Ask Maw for some money so we can go get some ices." Ali was the go to guy when it came to Maw. She had a soft spot for him and everybody thought it was because out of the four of us he was the only light skinned one.

Ali came back cheesing, "you know I always make things happen." "Whatever!" While I scoped the scenes on the streets, Ali kicked an empty bag of chips the whole two blocks we walked to the corner store. "Q, let me get a quarter" I looked to see T-Bone the local fiend begging for change as usual. "Hell No!" "You aint right young one Imma tell your motha." "Shit I won't even give her dope fiend ass a quarter let alone you T-Bone." "Ali, what about you" I looked at him and gave him the don't fuck with my money look. He looked down and said, "I can't."

The corner store on Gates and Nostrand had the best Italian Ices in Brooklyn. Plus the owner Maheer would occasionally hook us up because he had a crush on my mom, Nicky. Aint this about a bitch! I looked across the street and saw my brother Just rolling

3

dice at his real summer job. 'What's good Just?" "These nigga's money! Tell Maw dinner is on these nigga's tonight." The smile on Justice's face was priceless.

He had that smile that would make you either follow him or envy him. He looked just like my father. He inherited his dark chocolate complexion, broad shoulders, dark brown eyes and long dark eyelashes that the ladies loved and his coolie hair. There were about 20 dudes playing dice and slinging shit. I sat for a while watching my brother breaking niggas pockets 'til I got bored and walked into the corner store.

When I walked into the store Ali was talking to Maheer about school and shit. "What up Maheer let me get two lemon ices and one cherry?" Qahira liked the cherry because it would leave her lips red, making it look like she was wearing lipstick. "That will be $1.50. So Ali, how is your mother doing?" I looked over at dude. Ali was falling for the okey doke, like Maheer gave a fuck about him. The whole time was he just wanted to know how Nicky was.

It wasn't the first time some dude had asked about my moms. She was half Cuban and half black. She looked exotic and had a body that made even Just's friends try to get at her. The fucked up part was that Qahira was starting to look just like her. I don't really know Nicky like that. Out of all of us the only one that had any memories with her was Just. On a rare occasion he would tell us stories about her and my pops but for the most part he didn't fuck with her.

My pops had died right after Ali was born and I guess after that my mom's had went a little crazy and dropped the four of us at my grandmother's. Since then she had been getting high and we only seen her when my grandmother got her check or she needed bail money for getting caught boosting.

"Ali let me get some Lemon Heads." "I don't have no more change you know Maw don't go to work till this afternoon." I poked my head out the door to ask Just for some bread. Since he was being really flashy who knows how much he would come off of.

"Just! Just! Let me get some money? Maw only sent us with $1.50 and you know she don't go to work till this afternoon." He pointed my way and blew on the dice and said "this is for you little brother." I started walking towards him when I was pushed to the ground. I heard two shots and watched my brother's body crumple and drop. I felt the splatter of warm blood on my face and watched in disbelief as a pool of blood formed underneath his body. From that moment on, I felt like I was moving in slow motion. I grabbed Just's limp body and cradled him like a baby. The same way he held me when I was child. All those many nights when he was there to comfort and make me feel protected. I held him, I kissed his forehead and prayed for him. I wanted him to go heaven just like he deserved. The tears rolled down my face and I didn't move until the paramedics pried my brother body out my hands to put us both in the ambulance.

I was covered in so much blood that the ambulance took us both to Kings County Hospital. They weren't sure if I had also been shot.

After that I day I was no longer the carefree Q I had been. I was forced to step up for my family, they needed me. My youth died with Justice. It was time for me to become a man.

I hadn't thought about Just since he passed but watching Jul fighting for her life in the ICU brought back all those memories. My life was supposed to be changing and here I was all my demons were catching up to me. I yearned to kissed my baby girl lips and feel her touch.

I remembered the first time we met. It was Spring Break in Miami. She was with about 15 girls. Some of the baddest chicks you have ever seen in all sizes and shades. But Jul was shitting on all of them.

"Yo, pass the blunt" I looked back at Loc and contemplated giving him my shit. Suko kept driving and smirked. We had stopped smoking after that nigga after he told us about eating some girl's ass that had been grouped by the crew. That nasty nigga!

I was in a zone thinking about my new business venture and listening to some new young dude spitting fire lyrics, and repping the blocks where I was from. About 30 of us from MD, DC PA and NY decided at the last minute to jump on the highway and go to Miami. I usually liked driving my own shit but Suko had just copped a new Bentley so you know that nigga was coming through straight fronting.

"Taj, I'm not doing nothing, damn! I just need a break before my baby girl comes... Nah I'm not staying with Quron... I understand." His pregnant wife couldn't stand me. Nah, she fucked with me but she didn't trust me since I had fucked half her friends. Ha, ha ha! You know how it is. All these bitches swear they have that magic pussy to tame a dude. I was there to prove them wrong. The one chic I really wanted to get at was her sister that was in law school. I loved a girl that had a mind and was into building her own money. I saw her a couple of times when we threw parties but I never approached her because I wasn't ready for all that shit. I was still young and loved new pussy.

We arrived at the hotel and heard a familiar voice saying, "Yo, make sure my shit got them thick towels and a nice bathrobe because there is no way I am paying this much for some bullshit". I walked into hear my man Rod from BMore talking shit to the blond blue eyed young white lady behind the counter. "What up?" She looked at one of us to save her. Her face said please one of yah have to like white girls. "Loc, go get your mans," I laughed. "Rod, I got you." Loc pulled up close to oh girl, "baby girl you too pretty to be at this job all stressed out." Loc would sleep with anything. He was not choosy and didn't have no shame about it. A Jennifer Anniston look alike would not even get a second glance from me unless she was built like Coco she needed to be thick with a fat ass and I want to fuck you eyes.

I walked outside to breathe in that Miami air while I waited my turn to check in. It looked like it would be a while. "Excuse me," I looked and saw the prettiest manicured feet and thick calves. Her skin was glistening and mesmerizing. I followed her legs up to see thick thighs and a tattoo peaking from underneath her dress. That tat was a chain of diamonds, rubies and emeralds leading up to what I am guessing must have been a beautiful kitty kat as well.

I looked up to see the face that belonged to the strapless black dress. Shorty's face to my surprise and pleasure she was beautiful. She looked like Pocahontas with the jet black hair and everything. "Excuse me!" "Huh!" "Excuse Me!" Embarrassed I moved over, "sorry baby girl." Damn shorty had caught me slipping. I watched her walk into the lobby and felt like a pervert watching her ass jiggle. She turned around, stared at me and smiled. Damn let me find out Miami was where it was at.

JULISA SANTANTA

I felt my cell phone vibrate and seen Mieko's name on the caller id. "I'm coming, Conio" (Damn). I just got on the elevator." I was dying to do me and had been unable to since I was sharing a room with Mieko. I was starting to feel edgy so I had made an excuse that I had forgotten my ID. On my way in I seen a real sexy brother chocolate about 6 feet 4 and built like he played ball. The way he carried himself it seemed like he had money. He must be one of the dudes out here that played for the Dolphins.

I saw so many stars out here but that was definitely not my style. Too much drama, plus I had my own money. Damn sexy was nice and still on my mind. As I waited for the elevator I watched the interaction between him and his friends. He didn't seem like the other dudes he was with, they seemed thirsty and trying to holla at anything walking.

I felt embarrassed that I was still watching him, this wasn't like me. My man was doing a 3 year bid on an aggravated assault charge and not once had I looked any other way. I think its because I knew that his time was short. I must be going stir crazy.

I was ready to go back to NY and we still had a couple more days, I was thinking about making some excuse and getting the fuck out of here. I mean damn, how many times can somebody go to a beach? I laughed to myself. Plus these uppity bitches were getting on my mother fucking nerves. This was supposed to be a fun trip. Me and my girls had come down to enjoy spring break almost like a pre-pre bachelorette party. Pito had proposed unofficially while he had been locked up but everybody knew don't ever go on the jail talk. It was inevitable that we would end up being married one day, we had been together since the 8th grade but had known each other all of our lives his mom and my mother were best friends and I guess you could say it naturally happened.

The elevator finally came and I tried to rush in before a Suge Knight look-a-like tried to get in with me. "Oh baby girl you wasn't gonna hold the elevator?" "I didn't see you!" "You rude as hell but you bad as shit!" I ignored his ass and watched the elevator move from floor to floor; the 5th floor couldn't come quick enough. I pretended to text so he would get the hint. I couldn't get out the elevator soon enough . When the door open I kept it moving, when I heard the dude say "by the way there is no telephone reception in the elevators." I laughed damn I've been in Miami too long.

I rushed into the bathroom and pulled my bottle out. I was so glad to finally get some alone time to make myself feel better. I felt the rush of the cocaine hitting my body. I checked myself in the full length mirror attached to the door and made sure there was no evidence touched up my lipstick , now I was ready to party.

QURON JACKSON

I walked back into the lobby to find Suko had just finished
checking in. "Did you see Mami that just came in?" "Yeah she
was bad." "Shorty right there is definitely bring home to Maw
material." He laughed, "What? I aint never heard you say some
shit like that before. I hear that."' I fucked with Suko. He was a
humble dude and had become my right hand when my brother
passed. We both came up fucked up, hungry to make money. As
soon as I got put on, I put him on. The only chink I could find in
his armor was the fact that he fell in love every other day. He was
on his 4th kid and first marriage. I was hoping Taji was finally a
good woman for him because the last two weren't shit. One of
them bitches even propositioned me with some pussy. Talk about
cruddy. I had been around some dudes that had no loyalty even
to their own family but not me, Loc and Suko from the beginning
we knew no money or woman could come between us.

I can't lie; I'm even embarrassed to say, after my brother passed
away I got on some grimy shit. I was robbing niggas left and right
and just shitting on dudes. It was against everything I stood for.
But fuck it, it was a growing experience. I hated the world for
taking away one of the only people that loved me. I was trying to
get to the bottom of what happened to my brother.

I was fourteen, feeling myself, and I just became the man of the house… and a monster. Ali was too soft, my father was dead and I was the only man left at Maw's house. I felt like I had nothing to lose. I had to make sure my family ate so I was going to do whatever it took to make that happen. During this time Suko stood by me. He cosigned whatever I did - wrong or right he was down for whatever. My little robbery shit didn't last long because after a couple of months of that dumb shit I met Davi, or should I say he recruited me.

Just's man Hakeem put me on as look out for his coke operation in the projects. Even though I wasn't making money like that, I didn't mind because while other cats were happy getting scraps I was watching everything, learning the game and waiting for my time to jump into action. I was playing lookout for a couple months now and the winter just hit. I just copped a new coat and boots for me, Qahira and Ali. It would be our first Christmas where we would get the stuff we really wanted. I made that happen.

I was headed up the block to relieve the a.m. shift when I noticed that the block was empty except for T-Bone strolling up the Ave. to cop. I turned around just in time to see T-Bone look over and give a signal to a white van that was parked at the corner. I watched the van head towards the spot and come to a screeching halt. I yelled up to Hakeem "YOOO 5-0!" But it was too late. Two big under cover officers had already thrown him against the building, reached into his pocket and pulled out the money that T-Bone just gave him. The smirk on the detective's face said it all, "I finally got your ass." I ran over to try to reach Hakeem before they could put him in the back of the paddy wagon.

"Fam, I'll let your peoples know what happened and I will make sure to come check you." He said "no doubt!" This was it. My plan was going to come into action. I headed back to the second spot Hakeem managed to let them know the news and make sure everything was running smoothly. "Yo! Hakeem just got arrested and left me in charge." I watched everybody look up from the spades game like I had lost my mind. I kept going. Fuck it! I had nothing to lose. Plus I knew I was smarter than all those dudes. I didn't miss a beat. "He wants us to change the block and go on plan B." I seen Damien's face turn to rage and seen the vein on his neck potrude, "What little nigga? You aint in charge. Who the fuck is you!?" "Look Damien, I am telling you what it is. You really think I'm a look-out or an apprentice? Come on. I know he would have put you on if that package wasn't short last week, but it was so I got this. You know me and Hakeem family. Plus you don't even know who to go to for the re-up. So who you think should be in charge?"

Even though it seemed suspect, I knew they'd go with the flow since nobody wanted the money to dry up. No connect, no money. It was what it was.

I knew it would be impossible to gain my respect just on 'say so'. I had to show that my young age didn't mean shit. First things first, I ran to Hakeem's mom house. "Ms. Sheryl they got Hakeem." I pulled out 500 dollars and gave it to her out my own stash. I knew she wouldn't question anything. She knew what Hakeem did and as long as the money came rolling in she wasn't going to question shit. "I will be there tomorrow for his bail hearing." "Ok Quron you are a good boy. I'm glad Hakeem has good friends."

The next morning at the bail hearing I sat with Hakeem's mom and waited for his case to be called. When he showed up I watched Ms. Sheryl tell him exactly what I had instructed her to say. He looked at me and gave me the ok. It took less than 5 minutes for the judge to set bail and for Hakeem to realize that Detective Fox had not only got him on his sale to TBone, but the state also had numerous secret indictment charges. I watched as the light went out of Hakeem's eyes.   At the age of eighteen, the reality was with those charges he could be in prison his whole adult life.

After court I had Ms. Sheryl drop me off in front of the spot just in case anyone had any doubts. Being the only person that went to court made everything I said seem legit.

It was time to get dirty. I was either going to let my fear overcome me or I was going to do whatever it took to make money. Money was my first and only choice. I made my way down Broadway under the Z train where I knew I could cop a pistol with no questions asked. Even though I was only fourteen, it didn't matter. In Brooklyn, money always talked. I bought a snub nose .38 because it was small, left no shells and would still do the job.

I crawled in to the dirty cardboard box that T-Bone called home and laid down waiting on T-Bone to come back. I was dressed in old dirty work clothes that Maw saved from before my Grandpops passed. I sat in that filth watching mice and all kinds of shit crawl by. After what seems like hours T-Bone finally showed. He crawled into feel the .38 on his forehead I was ready to body him but before I could he swatted the gun out my hand.

Having no experience I panicked and wrestled him for the gun. Both of us fought with desperation of what was sure to come. T-Bone and I wrestled punching and squirming each of us knowing that the last person on the concrete would be the one to go to the grave. I reached in my sock and grabbed my knife and kept stabbing him on the arm of the hand he had wrapped around my neck. Finally after what seemed like hours he let go, moaning like a wounded dog.

I grabbed the .38 and put it to his head. "No son! I am someone's father. Please! I know your momma!" I looked down at him and for a split second my conscious told me don't do it - - but I had to come too far. It was not personal. It was business.

I had put that life behind me for a while but it seemed like when you trying to stop the crime they always bring you back in. My trip to Miami was a treat to myself because I was trying to get legit and only had a couple of months before I would be out of New York. I was 25 and had been in the game for 10 years and 6 months. In the drug game this was considered an eternity. I had lived a life of three men. I saw and did things people only read about. It was time. I was ready to finally move into my house in Maryland and take my grandmother and whatever family wanted to move with me.

So when I met Jul's in Miami, she caught a nigga at the right time. The streets had taught me to watch people and learn what they were hiding and that everybody had a weakness. She carried herself proper even when Rod had been a thirst bucket. She had on the new season's Loubotin's and her tennis bracelet was filled with quality diamonds. She seemed respectable, yet arrogant like money didn't impress her. I listened to her conversation and acted like I had no clue what she was saying. I had learned Spanish when I started dealing directly with the connect. Shit you always want to make sure you are ahead of the game. That was one of those secrets that you kept in your arsenal until you needed it.

I felt fucked up that I hadn't approached her but promised myself that she wouldn't catch me a slipping a second time if I had the opportunity. Damn, I was tripping. All these beautiful women and I'm stuck on oh girl. I sounded like Suko... nah never that. I took a nap and got dressed in my new pin striped, custom made grey suit. I met my mans and them down stairs to start the vacation off.

When I hit the lobby Loc was already there talking shit to the same girl at the front desk and Suko was on the phone with Taj. I already knew the deal Suko was going to have to report every 20 minutes what he was doing and Loc was going to fuck everything walking. Same shit just a different town. "Yo, I thought you said it was exclusive and yah niggas wearing Jeans and Polos". "Nah usually it is but Loc fucking some girl at this other spot so we hitting that up instead." I refused to change even though I was overdressed. I never looked average and I didn't give a fuck what niggas thought. If they smelled money or thought they could come get this money they would get a nice surprise when my .357 made their body limp.

"Loc, they searching nigga's." "Of course but let me handle that." From the outside the club looked like a warehouse that had been converted into a night club. We walked up to a line that was at least two blocks long. The ladies had on outfits that made niggas pay bills. Suko, Loc and I were escorted in as you heard a hater say "Yo, who is that, why you letting them in?" This caught the ladies' attention. They saw long money.

The club was packed and the DJ was killing it. "Imma go to the bar. You want something?" "Get me a bottle of Ciroc." "Alright, I got u." "Damn yah can't wait until the table service comes", Loc chimed in. "Nah I just want to see what's popping on the other side." As I walked to the bar I caught the eye of three ladies watching me. They were looking thirsty like they knew a nigga was getting it.

"Pardon me ma." The best looking of the bunch gave a face like she was tired of hearing game and was trying to dismiss me. "What you looking at me like that for? I am talking to the bartender." "Oh. I'm sorry I thought you were one of these lame dudes that have been trying to holla at me all night." I ignored her and went around her inching closer to the bar giving her and her girls my back. She tapped my shoulder to get my attention. I ignored her ass, she was cute but somebody had swelled her head. Just because she was light skinned with green eyes didn't mean shit to me. "Excuse me," I turned around to find shorty dying for some attention.

"So what is your name?" "Q" "Hi Q, I'm Celeste." I turned back around to order my drink. "Can I get a Grand Marnier and a bottle of Ciroc." "How does Grand Marnier taste." "It's smooth but strong." I paused and looked at her knowing quite well that if I wasn't playing cool I would have said like my dick. "Where you from?" "Brooklyn." One of her bird friends giggled, " I told you, they always from New York." I grabbed my bottles and turned around "you ladies have a good night." I smirked as I walked away leaving Celeste with her mouth open she wasn't used to anyone playing her. I knew she would come find me.

That was the difference between some of these high maintenance chicks and my block chicks. They wanted to hear the same game just sugar coated whereas my block chicks respected hearing the real shit. I tended to stick with my shorties from the block. There was no frontin. I said how I felt and it was ok no matter how vile I came out my mouth.

My man Loco had looked out and got us a table in the VIP section. I sat next to Suko and gave my man Loc the pound. I quietly contemplated the scene and realized that this VIP shit was for the birds half these niggas in the VIP section were frontin for these bobble head bitches that were just as broke as they were. This shit did not impress me.

Just as I was about to go out in the crowd, I felt somebody watching me and turned around to see shorty from the bar. "Hey, where did you go? I thought you were going to let me taste that Grand Marnier." She was smiling like she was on a tooth paste commercial. I just looked at her as she sat her uninvited ass down. Loco looked at me and just shook his head. "So how do you like Miami?" "It's alright." "I am from Atlanta." She told me how she had moved down here because her baby daddy played for the Dolphin's and how when he got up here he had gotten on some Hollywood shit. She was mixed with Trinidadian and Italian and couldn't stand that people always thought she was Spanish. We talked for about 20 minutes and by the time we finished she was ready to get out of there.

"Q, why don't we get out of here and go to my place and get comfortable this club is weak anyways." I thought about it. Fuck it, I had plenty of nights to go to the clubs. I was already tired from the trip so chilling in some pussy and laying back didn't sound too bad. I gave my man the heads up and proceeded to walk out of the place. "Give me a minute ok, I need to go to the bathroom and tell my girls I will see them tomorrow." I played the wall and finished my bottle waiting for Shorty.

"Papi," I turned to see who was in my face. My mouth dropped as I saw shorty from the hotel. "Sweetie, hold my purse." Surprised, I grabbed her bag. "I need to fix my bra." I watched her adjust herself. "So first you push me out of the way and now you got me holding your bag. Damn that is how you treat a fly dude like me?" She smirked "of course not". She grabbed her purse, "thanks."

She had on a sexy strapless dress that came up to her thighs. I caught a hint of baby powder and cocoa butter lotion. On her back was a tattoo that said 'Julisa'. She had her hair silky black her out. She was so damn sexy. You could see her perky breast through the dress. She had a diamond anklet and her feet where French manicured. "I am sorry. I'm Julisa.. but everybody calls me Jul." "Q."

"Q you smell real nice, what is that?" "Something exclusive my man made for me." I made a mental note that I was going to have to pay my Muslim connect some more money. I had asked him to make something that would make the ladies in Miami drop them drawers and if this worked on Jul he was about to get a bonus.

Out of nowhere Julisa got real close and planted a kiss on my neck. I turned around thinking that the whole scene was suspect and looked around for the setup. Even though my mind was fucked up the kiss made my man instantly rise to attention. I felt her soft lips touch my ear as she whispered "roll with me." I turned around to see a duffy nigga roll up. He was dressed in suit and looked like he definitely didn't belong at this party and if he was there by invitation he was someone's lawyer or something.

"Hey Julisa, how are you?" "I am fine Trevor, how are you?" Trevor this is my man Q. Q this is my classmate Trevor." Trevor sized me up to see if he could take me then looked away like he knew the deal. "Nice meeting you." I just gave the nigga the nod. I didn't know who this clown was so fuck this dude. He looked at Julisa and uncomfortably eyed her from head to toe. After a moment of silence he must have gotten the hint because he excused himself and told Julisa he would see her in class. "Sorry about that. Trevor is my local stalker. I swear he followed me here. I can't even see him leaving New York for Spring Break." We both laughed. "Oh you from NY?" She smiled, "where else."

"Excuse me, Q" I heard Celeste's voice. "Are you ready to go?" Damn, I looked at Jul wishing our conversation hadn't have to end so soon. I watched as Jul and Celeste both gave each other the "I am the shit" look. I was pissed I had fucked up. I got caught up too early. Now I was stuck with Celeste for the night. I didn't even introduce them, there was no need. Celeste grabbed my hand and started heading to the front door as if saying, "bitch he is going home with me." Jul pulled me back and gave me another hug, "Thanks. I will see you at the hotel tomorrow." Celeste looked like she could have stabbed her right then. I grabbed Jul's phone from out of her hand and dialed my number making sure it registered on my phone. I told her "I will call you tomorrow." She just watched me and smirked knowing I just turned the tables.

Celeste drove a black Benz- an older model coupe. She still had the factory rims on so I knew although she thought she was getting money, she was doing only slightly better than the average chick. We drove 15 minutes on the highway as I made a mental note to see where I was in case some shit popped off. Many cats got caught up with their pants down... but not this one. We drove into a gated community. Her house was a nice size.

We walked in the front door and there was a big picture of her wrapped in a black mink with what gave the appearance of nothing underneath. "Are you hungry baby?" "Nah I am good." "I am going to go grab us something to drink." I sat down on her brown leather couches and looked around at her African Art and Dolphin's memorabilia. Her baby daddy was definitely still hitting it. She came in with a glass of wine and a Heineken. "I will be right back get comfortable." I turned on the TV and caught up on the Knicks highlights on ESPN. 5 minutes later she came down in a pink bikini and two towels in her hand. She actually had a sexier body naked then I thought. She looked a little skinny for my taste but when she got undressed she had nice thighs, some hips and big ass for her frame.

"Let's go baby." I got up. I was always down for whatever. I followed her to the back of the house and walked between the sliding doors to a pool house. "You feel like swimming?" I kicked my shoes off, took off my suit and threw them on the back of the chair. I had on my boxers and my piece. She jumped in the pool and smiled, "you are one sexy man". I walked to the stairs entering the pool, took my boxers off and laid my gun on top. I wasn't trying to go home in wet drawers. I watched her eyes as she looked at my man and could tell she was excited.

The pool was heated it felt nice. I swam towards her. I didn't come here to play. I came to have fun. I grabbed her from behind and pinned her against the pool wall and rubbed her from behind. I lifted up her wet hair kissed her neck and massaged her kitty. She moaned. I felt her body tense up and saw goose bumps appear on her arms.

"Daddy hold on, you are going to make me cum before we even get started." She turned around and went under the water and started kissing my dick. I don't know if it was the water because I have had plenty of head but this chick was an expert. She came up for air and went back down but after a few minutes she came up and said "damn, do you ever cum". I laughed. " I can't come like that." I grabbed her hand and walked towards the pool stairs. I grabbed my piece and followed her in the house.

I followed shorty up the stairs to her room. Even though she was just making ends meat you could tell she hustled a couple of dudes to come out their pockets. I entered her room and she pushed me on her bed. She was real demanding. She pulled my dick out from underneath the towel and started massaging it and smacking it on her face. She slowly placed her warm mouth on my balls and started sucking on them slowly.

She looked up at me and licked her lips and turned around and grabbed her ankles standing up and spread her pussy for me to look at. I stood up and grabbed the condom out of my pants pocket she turned around and took the condom from me. She placed it in her mouth and slid it on my dick. I got behind her and entered her slowly and began to grind her rhythmically. I pushed in slowly to try to put my dick all the way in.

"'No" she moaned "it's too much, take your time". I pulled my dick out of her wet pussy. I laid flat on the bed and she mounted me. She began to grind on my dick real slow. She moved as if she was dancing on my dick. The wetter she got, the deeper it went in. The deeper my dick drove in, the harder the thrust got.

I heard a moan escape her mouth as she dug her nails deep in to my chest and I saw her cum drip down my dick onto my balls. She got off, pulled off the condom and sucked my dick until I released. Swallowed me dry… I guess I can cum that way.

We both fell asleep, satisfied.

I heard the faint sound of my cell phone ringing in what seemed like a dream. "Yo!" "Nigga get up." It was my brother Ali, "what's up". "They got Qahira." "Who got Qahira?" "I don't know somebody just called my cell phone talking about I had 2 days to get 500 stacks or I wouldn't see my sister." I jumped up "I am on my way."

I woke Celeste up and told her I had business to take care of and needed her to take me back to the hotel. On the way to the telly I was already making calls. I let Loc and Suko know what was happening and made some calls to Brooklyn. It was a big city but everybody that was in the streets knew each other. I put my peoples on a mission. The streets would talk. These niggas would not get away with fucking with my family. They had a 50 thousand dollar bounty on their head and there was no loyalty when it came to money.

I was confused by this whole shit. Why would they take Qahira? Why would they call Ali? He's not even built like that. Anybody that knew anything would know he aint got that kind of bread. My mind was racing. I was from the hood. I knew niggas would not let Qahira go so there was no way I was paying the ransom. Somebody must have gotten it mistaken. Just because I was hibernating from the streets did not mean I was not the same killer. I wasn't worried about finding the dudes because I've seen people sell they family for a quarter of the money I was offering. I was just worried that my sister would not come back breathing. I took the first flight from Miami to NY and had Suko bring my piece back since it wasn't registered I wouldn't be able to bring it back on the plane.

The two hour flight felt like two days. I stepped out of the airport and saw Davi's Rover parked on the curb. "What up? Any news!" "Yeah we have two dudes that might be involved with this shit with your sister. I got my people posted up at their hide out right now waiting on you to give the word." "No doubt. Let's go."

I told you Brooklyn wasn't but so big. Considering my reputation in the drug game and with Davi's help, information came really quick. It turns out one of the dudes involved was a talker. He ran his mouth at the barbershop in front of one of our runners. He had the balls to brag about how he had a setup that was guaranteed money on some ransom shit. Since reward money was on the line the runner gladly gave dude up.

The spot was in Upstate New York so not only would it take us a while to get there but we had to be extra careful. Some of the most racist police were up there. We could fuck around and catch a charge before we even did shit. The house was in the middle of

24

nowhere, no neighbors around for miles. There was no real security set up except for a couple guys sitting outside the house monitoring the area; these niggas must not have known who they was fucking with -- or really thought nobody would find them out here.

We pulled up to the lookout spot where Davi's goons were and got out. They had already been posted for the last couple of hours so they were able to see how the spot was setup and how many people were involved. They had only seen three dudes guarding the spot. One that smoked every 20 minutes, one that occasionally came outside to use his cell phone and the other one hadn't been visible since they had come in.

The last time they had seen Qahira was when they came to the spot and at that time they had reported she was gagged, blind folded and had her hands cuffed behind her back. Davi and I decided to sit and scope out the scene before we came up with a game plan. I couldn't even concentrate on a game plan. Waiting had me fucked up. They did the ultimate by fucking with my family. I wanted every nigga that was involved dead.

"D, I am not playing no games, I am just going in clapping shit up." "Nigga are you crazy? We have at least a two hour ride back home. We need to play this right. Q, you ain't thinking right. These punks are just pawns. You need to find a way to get to the King and the best way to do that is through his Queen. Listen Q, what we going to do is this; My man said that there had been a shorty that came up here looking like she was running shit. She was really flashy. Diamonds and the whole nine. So I am thinking either she put this together or she knows who did. My other mans and them followed her and an older woman to a nail shop and waiting on our next step."

I thought about what Davi had said and hated the fact that ladies were involved. Even thinking about putting my hands on one had me fucked up. I got out the car and even though I didn't smoke cigarettes I copped a puff from one of the goons. This shit was crazy these niggas had my back against the wall but it was my family or theirs. I got back in the car. "D, we good let's do this."

When I got to the spot Shorty and her mom's had been bound and gagged. The older woman was whimpering and shaking while the younger one was confident like she was used to this and showed no fear about her present situation. Since the younger one was rocking like she was hard she would feel my wrath first.

I gently moved her hair from her eyes and whispered in her ear, "if you want to live past today you will answer my questions and do exactly as I say". I yanked the tape off her mouth and asked her how many people are inside. She stayed quite. I grabbed her hair and asked her again this time with the tip of my knife on her forehead. "Fuck you nigga you done fucked up, you fucking with the wrong bitch. Do you know who I am? I am Pedro's wife." "I don't give a fuck whose wife you are but what I do know is that I will kill both you bitches."

The older woman started to cry uncontrollably making the younger one pissed and come out her mouth sideways about what her husband was going to do. I slit her face in a Z shape and as the blood started to flow, she started talking. After that I guess she figured the more information she gave, the better her odds would be to be kept alive.

We had Shorty's mom still at the spot and made shorty make the call letting them know she was on the way back the ransom had been paid and not to touch Qahira until she got there. Before we could approach the house the door opened. The same cat that smoked was coming out for what would be his last puff. He struck a match to light his cigarette as he went to light it my gun rose and a shot entered his mouth and exited the back of his head. His body dropped.

The loud noise of the gunshot made the others come out blazing. According to shorty they were 6 mother fuckers all together. I used her as a vest and felt the bullets tear through her body. I took cover behind the car. My goons were already set up on both sides of the house and ready to ambush anybody that ran out the front. There were two niggas left.

I circled around the back as one of the dudes was pulling Qahira in the car. Knowing I had a clear shot I let out three bullets to his back. Qahira fell to the ground as the driver sped off knocking down everything in his path. I shot the back windshield and started running towards the car, but he had already fishtailed around the corner and driven up the main road. I watched the taillights until I couldn't see them making me more pissed off that this nigga had gotten away.

Reality hit me when I heard faint police sirens, Davi had already grabbed Qahira and threw her in the back seat so I jumped in the ride and we sped off heading to BK. Qahira was so scared she wouldn't let me go. After almost an hour she had finally calmed down enough to get some sleep.

"Yo D, good looking." "Q, you know we fam." Even though I knew a lot of people growing up and chilled with a whole bunch of dudes when it came to grimy shit, I didn't fuck with just anybody. Davi was the one that had put me on and always had my back no matter what. He was my connect's son. It felt like a short period of time since we had first met but it was going on ten real thorough years.

Davi and I had met after I positioned myself at the head of the corner. I had promised Hakeem that I would kill the snitch which would mean that he would come home but on the strength that I would be his right hand. Since I knew him and his right hand were already beefing I knew it would be easy to slide right in. I was fourteen feeling myself I had just become the man of the house. I had placed myself at the head of the corner and had taken someone's life.

I felt like I had nothing to lose. I had to make sure my family ate so I was going to do whatever it took to make that happen. Although people may talk about how hard they were, catching a body trumped all of that. I gained my respect so I went from walking with the best new Jordan's to getting dope fiends to rent me cars when I didn't even have a license. My closet was full of clothes and Qahira and Ali didn't want for nothing.

I was headed to Hakeem to make sure that everything was cool and everybody was doing what they needed to be doing when I heard niggas yell, "Slim!" Slim was that dude that was a menace to young brothers trying to make money. He had no respect for anybody that was younger than him and felt his reputation had earned some kind of fear amongst us young heads.

Slim walked past me and rolled up on Hakeem, "come off that right now." "Yo Slim I can't I have to pay my connect and it can't be short." "Nigga I don't give a fuck who you got to pay. I want my cut now." While Hakeem contemplated which was the worse fate, Slim grew more and more pissed that this young kid didn't know what he was about. Slim grabbed his .45 and started gun butting Hakeem. Since Slim was much bigger than Hakeem his attempts to fight back just made him slip and fall and along with him went the gun. Everybody else had walked away watching from afar not wanting to be the next victim. I stood next to Hakeem and grabbed the gun that had slid underneath a parked car and pointed it at Slim.

"Little nigga what do you think you doing drop my shit right now." I stood with the .45 ready to shoot. "Little Nigga did you hear me I will beat your fucking ass drop the gun right now. Listen nigga you don't want me to drop you like I did your brother you better give me my shit."

I let off three shots inhaling the smoke escaping the nozzle. I shot him twice, once in the chest and once in the face. Even though I knew he was dead I continued to kick and choke the nigga like he was going to get up.

I stood there mad as the streets scattered. "Yo, get in." I turned around and seen a Spanish looking dude in a Honda Accord with the door open. "You hear me get in." I contemplated running and getting caught by 5.0, but since I had nowhere to go. I jumped in. I watched him look at me as we both sat quite heading towards my crib. Finally he spoke, "Young God, they call me Davi." I just nodded my head. "You don't know who I am but I have been watching you. I like the way you handled yourself back there." I just nodded.

He went on to tell me how he had been scoping the block for his peoples, and they were looking to expand business and were looking for a couple of soldiers. He said Hakeem worked for him but it had been questionable whether or not he was built for a takeover. I sat there in a daze half listening the other thinking about what I had just done. I had just killed the man that had killed my brother. Even though I dreamed that one day I would find out the truth. I hadn't been ready to ask questions about Just because I knew I didn't want to know until I was ready to handle that person myself.

"Yo, are you listening?" I looked over. "I said, are you scared to make money?" "Nah," I shook my head, I couldn't even hear him anymore. I guess he must have felt it because he stopped talking and turned up the music. We rode in silence. I felt the bass fill my whole body until we hit my block. When he came to a stop, I grabbed the door handle to get out. "Wait a minute young god," he went into the back seat and grabbed a track phone and handed it to me. "We will be in touch." I got out the car and seen Maw walking up the street with groceries in her hand.

I grabbed the bags. "Maw why didn't you catch a cab with the money I gave you." "No baby I don't use that money. You think I don't know what you doing, you aint got know business hanging out with those older boys. It aint right. If you don't get it together they going to kill you, you betta get Jesus in your life Quron before it's too late. One of these days my prayers won't be enough." I looked away I wanted to ask Maw would god forgive me for killing two men when I was just 16.

Here we were 10 years later and we are still riding together. On our way home from the chaos Davi had asked me if I minded if he could make a stop and grab his little sister and drop her off at the Correctional Facility. Although Qahira was worn out and I had, had a long day who was I to refuse after all he had done for my sister? I hated coming anywhere close to a jail and felt antsy getting close to something that could potentially have me caged the rest of my life.

JULISA SANTANA

"D, thanks for picking me up." "No problem C Chip you know it's nothing." "Q and Qahira this is my sister Jul." "How yah doing?" I turned around to introduce myself and who do I see? Sexy from the nightclub in Miami. Damn. Small world. I acted like I never saw dude before. Besides he was with someone and I wasn't trying to blow nobody up. I also wasn't sure what his connection was to Davi so I played my position and stayed quite.

"I can't believe you cut your vacation short for a VI." I looked at Davi surprised he would be telling my business to strangers and decided to let it go since there seemed to be a lot of tension in the car. Who was this dude that Davi was feeling extra comfortable in front of? I am going to have to find out.

"D, unlike those birds you deal with I can do a bid. I've done so for three years strong so 2 more months will not kill me." He dropped me off at the bus stop for my regular Saturday visit. Not trying to be rude, I turned around to say bye to sexy and his girl. It seemed as if it was only the two of us in the car as we stared at each other, like were looking into each other souls. Davi's voice brought me back,

"C Chip I will be here at 5 so don't marinate around doing dumb shit." I looked away from sexy and said bye to his girl. I grabbed my bag and walked away feeling crazy like I had just cheated on Pito for the first time.

Pito and I have been together since we were 14 years old. We have known each other all our lives. His mom and my moms are best friends. My father doesn't like Pito but deals with our relationship on the strength of my mother. He is in jail for an aggravated assault with a deadly weapon charge. In the past 8 years he had been in an out of jail. His temper always managed to get him caught up in dumb stuff and his pride always takes him over the top.

I hated coming to this place. Every time I came I felt violated. It felt as if they were making the family pay for the inmate's mistakes. By the time they made you take off items they felt were unacceptable, go through metal detectors and get searched, you were worn out before the visit.

I sat down and waited for Pito to come down. I looked around to see women and kids waiting for an inmate. I hated to see children in this environment. It was going on an hour and still, no Pito. "Excuse me officer I have been sitting here waiting for at least an hour and my boyfriend still has not come down." The woman correctional officer looked me up and down and laughed.

"Maybe he doesn't want to come down or he's not even thinking about you since his time is almost up." She looked over at her coworker, another plain looking woman whom just turned away, slightly embarrassed. I walked away and sat back down. I knew how these CO's could be. They wanted a reason to mistreat my man and I refused to give it to her. I knew she wouldn't be talking that shit if we were on the streets. What pissed me off was the extra interest in my man and that she knew his time was short.

Two hours later I was fuming I seen that same CO smirking and looking at me so I refused to give her any ammo. I just smiled and kept waiting for my man. 15 minutes later my man showed up at the door, our visit was almost ½ way over. As soon as I saw him it made everything better. He was one of those guys that women flocked to he was 5' 11' light skinned, with hazel eyes he looked like he could have been a model. Pito also had a nice ass body. Being in out the pen, he always made sure he hit the weights.

It was tough being in a relationship with him sometimes. There were always some inappropriate bitches. On the visits half these whores couldn't stop looking. If they knew how good he could lay the pipe they would be on him even more. But he was my man and no matter how many trials and tribulations we always made it through. These visits held me until the next visit.

"Hey Pa, what's good." "What up?" "What is wrong with you?" "Why you late?" "Pito what are you talking about I have been here since this morning." "So why they just calling me." "I don't know did something go on, because that CO on the left the brown skinned one has been giving me shit all visit." He looked over at both CO's and looked away. "Those chicks are crazy they are on my dick that's all. Fuck them chicks I didn't come down here to talk about them." Something was wrong I don't know what it was but he seemed uncomfortable and wouldn't look me in the face. Everything in my gut told me so but I played it cool.

"Baby I missed you; I can't wait for you to come home. I made reservations for us to go away for the weekend." "Yeah that's good." "I went and seen your mom's and brought her that money Lex gave me." He shook his head. "Yo what the fuck is the problem I just got off a plane cut my vacation short to come see you and you won't even look me in the eye you haven't even given me a kiss or showed no kind of love." "Jul you not in this fucking place, this is like living in hell. My time is short and I don't need this shit you really need to chill the fuck out before I walk out this v-i."

What was this nigga on? I sacrificed three years of my life and when his time was short he starts acting brand new? "I am sorry baby, I understand." "No you fucking don't this shit is mad stressful and you at Spring Break? Come the fuck on. You lucky I still fuck with you. Go home. I am done with this visit." He got up from the table and walked out the visiting room. I just sat dumbfounded I didn't know what happened but I knew that when he got out of here he would never talk to me like that or I would be locked up for cutting him myself.

I got up and refused to let them chicks see me cry. I smiled the best way I could and waived to them bitches and walked out. As soon as I hit the front door tears started rolling down my face. I sat to wait for Davi I didn't want to call him and let him know what was going on so I just waited for the visit to be over. The bell rang and people started coming out. I watched as one girl that looked real familiar kept watching me. She seemed like she was taking her time taking her stuff out of her locker and kept looking over at me. I looked away. This day couldn't get any worse where was Davi it was ½ an hour past five already and that was not like him being late.

"Excuse me, are you Jul," I turned around to see the same girl from the locker. "Yeah"! I don't know if you remember me, my name is Kiera. Pito and my man are codefendants, I met you at the trial." "Oh ok, how you doing." "Listen I know this ain't any of my business and all and I probably shouldn't be doing this but shit I would want somebody to tell me. You know the light

36

skinned C.O. that was with the other one that was riding you? Well, she is pregnant by Pito." "Excuse me!" "Yeah I am sorry to have to be the one to tell you this but I would have wanted to know." I usually wouldn't just believe any random chick but something in my gut was telling me that everything she was saying was the truth. At that point I didn't care who seen me break down the tears just started flowing. I didn't even know this girl and she knew more than enough about my man! I didn't question her or ask how she knew. It was all too much for one day. I was dying to get home and feel the relief that only coke could bring. Right now I needed it more than I needed air.

She gave me a hug and asked, "Are you ok?" I just nodded, "do you have a ride because if you need one I can bring you home." I managed to give her a half nod. "Let me leave this money and I will meet you in front to get on the bus." I quickly called Davi. I couldn't let him see me like this, it could cause real problems and my family wasn't the type to take shit like this lightly. If my family found out… Pito may not even make it off the island. As much as I was hurting and wanted to see him feeling my hurt, I didn't want somebody's death on my conscious.

"Hey D, where you at?" "I am leaving the town now I had to handle some shit for your father, I will be right there." "Don't worry about it I got a ride." "Are you sure?" "Yeah, it's Pito's codefendant's girlfriend." "Oh ok hit me up when you get home so I can know you got there safe." "I will." "Later!"

I can't remember the whole ride home it felt like I didn't breathe until I reached my dorm room. I just kept thinking about all the plans Pito and I had. We were supposed to have a baby. We were supposed to get married. I can't believe my first love, the love of my life, the one I had wasted all these years on had deceived me.

I wanted to make him pay. Was it my lack of sexual experience that had made him stray? Was this the first woman? I felt like I was going crazy with all the unknown reasons why he would do this to me!

I slept all day Saturday and Sunday and forced myself to get up for classes on Monday. I felt like I was in a trance. All week I wouldn't even answer my dorm door or cell phone. Two weeks passed and I felt like I was just floating. It was Tuesday and I was out of class due to a teacher's conference. I sat looking at the phone that had been ringing for the past ½ hour I was going to curse out whoever didn't get the hint that I just wanted to be left alone. I can't deal with no one else's shit right now.

"Heeelllo!" "Jul, where have you been your cell phone is off and I have been trying to call you since we got back from ATL I need you." "Ty I am going through some shit right now what is so important." "So am I, I am pregnant and" she paused "I don't know if it's Black or Julio's". "Are you fucking crazy Tynese? You are still pulling this dumb shit you are going to get someone killed?"

Tynese was having this triangular affair ever since High School. Now it was almost six years of this same crazy shit. If Black and Julio weren't tired of it, I sure was. Julio and Tynese have been together since 9th grade. In 11th grade they went through a little break up because Tynese decided that her future needed something more than an engineer husband, with two kids and a nice house.

During the breakup she met Black at the courts where all the ball players and hustlas hung out. He was an upcoming dude that was starting to get paper and was known as a no-nonsense type of nigga. After they had been together a year Tynese and Black were stopped by the police while driving home from the movies. The police found drugs in the car and locked them both up. Black

38

plead to the charges so that Tynese would be released. He spent two years in jail.

That was her wakeup call, for the moment, because she decide to go back to Julio. But she kept in contact with Black writing, visiting and putting money in his commissary during his bid. When Black came home she has been juggling the two. Julio and Black both denied they knew about each other but it went on so long it's almost as if they just accepted it – not without its crazy moments. They've shot at each other. Even started an all out brawl at the fish spot.

Now she was pregnant and didn't know who the father was. With a baby involved it would bring the drama to the next level. "So what are you going to do?" "What do you mean I have an appointment to get rid of it today at 3:00 p.m. will you take me?" I sat dumbfound "I got you. I am on my way."

"Take off your clothes put the gown on with opening in the back. The nurse will be in to take your vitals in the next couple of minutes." "Girl are your sure this is what you want to do." "No, Jul but I am here and unless I get a sign from up above I guess I am moving forward." I was praying that she wouldn't get rid of it. Me and Pito had a couple of pregnancies but after two failed miscarriages I figured I just couldn't have any kids. So I was hoping Tynese would have this baby, if only selfishly.

Knock, Knock! "Hi! I am Qahira your nurse." "Hey, don't I know you" I couldn't believe it. This was starting to get freaky. It was sexy's girlfriend. "Yeah, how you doing? Your friends with my brother Davi, right." "Actually my brother is I just met him that night." Oh so sexy was her brother. "Oh, that's your brother." "Yeah girl, do you really think I would have let you two stare each other down like that in my face." I blushed, "Nah no disrespect it was not like that". She smirked. Damn this was crazy it was the third time that me and sexy had linked up somehow or another I would have to give him a call at this point I was no longer with Pito and I had nothing to lose.

"So Tynese how are you feeling?" I turned around to see the reason that I had really come here. Ty was in a little ball tears falling down her eyes. "Girl are you ok." "I can't do this Jul." "You don't have to. I told I got your back." I silently thanked

God. He just had answered my prayers. Qahira grabbed Tynese's hand "Listen sweetie, you do what is best for you. Only you will be ok with your decision". All three of us sat in the room for the next 15 minutes talking and helping Ty through her next step. Qahira was real cool she even invited us to her brother's birthday party Saturday. I just might have to make an appearance.

QURON JACKSON

Weeks passed since that whole bullshit happened with Qahira and still no info on who Pedro was and how he had become interested in my paper. My man Davi was on it so I knew it wouldn't be long before I knew what was cracking. That dude was like the Feds. When they knew shit, they really knew shit. Since everything had happened Ali was acting really scary and Qahira, who was always a rider, was holding up well. She finally went back to the clinic to work this week.

Celeste had been blowing my phone up but I hadn't returned any of her calls. I don't know what she thought was going to happen. She lived miles away and even though she could suck a real good dick, I never wife bitches that fucked niggas on the first night. Too bad my dick took over I could have been laid up with Spanish shorty. The fucked up part was she was Davi's sister. I already had 99 problems and I wasn't about to make a bitch one.

I had been playing it low key from the blocks. From maw's house to home again. I wasn't feeling like entertaining until I knew who this nigga Pedro was so it had been a minute since I had really hung out with my peoples.

But today I would have to break that. My man Suko was having a baby shower for his wife. Although she couldn't stand me because I had fucked half her bird friends and treated them like the freaks they were, I was still the baby's godfather. I made a stop at the boutique where they were registered but by the time I got there everything on the registry was bought. I decided to make my gift a little more personal and stopped at Budo's my Jeweler. I got my god daughter a pair of diamond earrings and necklace.

As I pulled up to Suko's spot in New Jersey I pulled around back to the backyard to see over 100 guests. They went all out on this event. This was his fourth kid but his wife's first.

I knew it was going to be a long night when the first person I saw was Bugs. He's Suko's cousin and the neighborhood pest. Always trying to be down, but a little slow. The scariest kind in the book - a mentally disabled gangsta. He would do any trick to entertain you. From break dancing on the corner to busting somebody shit open just because we put the battery in his back. He was family though so nobody else could fuck with him except Suko, Loc and me. Everybody else was scared to even call him out his name.

"What up Bugs?" "Oh shit, yo it's my man Q what up, what up, what up." "Chilling how you been." "Good you know how it is always in the street making money." Bugs sells dime bags that he doesn't even know I supply for him. I couldn't let him know because he is a talker. Who knows what someone can get out of him. I sold smoke to all the local niggas just to keep my money recycling back to me. My real hustle was selling that weight to the same niggas that couldn't stand me but needed me.

"Q this is my wifey, Essence" I looked over to see a big boned shorty that had on a tight little shirt that looked like it belong to one of her kids and a mini skirt and sandals with the meat from her feet coming out the shoe. "What up?" She looked at me like I was a snickers bar. Trifling ass whore. "What up Q, I heard about you?" "That's what's up. Well let me go see Taj and Suko since I am already late." "Ok I will see you later." I look over at shorty and said "nice meeting you". She grabbed my hand and jerked it like a dick "nice meeting you to". Don't get me wrong. I have dealt with some thick girls and they have had some good pussy. But they were classy chicks going to school, not Bugs' sloppy seconds.

I laughed. Sometimes bitches swear they can just fuck anybody because they have a pussy. That was Q at 17 not 25. I walked around and seen a couple niggas I knew and gave hugs to some of the QV's as Loc would call them -- Quron's Victims. I finally got to the guest of honors Taj and Suko. "What up Suk? This is real nice! How you doing mama you looking beautiful as ever?" "Hmmm Hmmmm why you came so late Quuuron? You were caught up in something?" "Nah Taj I was getting my little god daughter something that she deserves and won't ever have to get from any nigga but her god father and her father." "Yeah and what is that?" "Diamonds!" She opened the box and started smiling "Thanks Q, Brianna will definitely love this gift." Suko laughed "Brianna or her mama".

I felt my celly buzzing and grabbed it to see who was calling. It was my man Davi. "Yo, what's good?" "What's up? Can you meet me?" "I am at this baby shower and shit." "How long?" "Meet me in an hour at the spot." "No doubt I will see you there." I finished chilling with my people ate a plate and a piece of cake, had some champagne and headed out to meet Davi.

The spot was a brownstone in Manhattan that belonged to Davi's other lady. She was a real pretty Asian chick with the phattest ass you would ever see and the prettiest green eyes. She was so on point I didn't even know her name or had even spoken more than

44

two words to her. And that time it was to let me know Davi was running behind and did I want something to drink. After that she was always either upstairs or in the back. I don't really think Davi trusted niggas so I felt honored that he had trusted me in his space. That dude was real private. You never knew what to expect.

I remember seeing him one time with a real pretty Spanish chick and two little girls at Great Adventures. He just nodded like he didn't know me. Later on he told me not to take it personal but the streets were the streets and family was family. I respected that and fucked with him because of that.

I rang the doorbell and looked around to see Davi's Bentley parked two doors up. I chuckled. Part of the reason that nigga was no longer driving the Honda was because of the money I made him and he in turned helped me make. I turned around to see one of Davi's goons looking at me like I was crazy. He let me in to the front living room where they had the most explicit Italian leather and Egyptian statues. I sat and waited next to the waterfall that was located next to the patio door.

After about five minutes Davi came out in a bathrobe and house slippers. "What up Q?" "What's up?" "How is Qahira?" "She is good you know holding up." "Good, Good, Good. Listen I didn't mean to disturb you at the baby shower and all but I figured what I needed to tell you was serious."

Davi looked over at the goon. "Grab me that envelope in my briefcase." The goon came back with what looked to be a large manila envelope. "Now give me some privacy because I need to speak to my man."

I felt like what Davi was about to tell me would somehow change me -- and not in a good way. "Listen Q, you know you are my man's and all. When I found out this information believe me I didn't want to bring this to you until I knew that it was true. So here it goes…"

"The way that Pedro got to you is because he fucks with your brother. I was told that him and your brother have been seeing each other for about a year. They were pillow talking when your name came up. Your brother was boasting and telling the nigga about who you were and how your paper was long. So dude got excited and tried to make moves on your paper."

I was stuck for a minute, speechless. I was so pissed I could feel the heat rising making the vein on my forehead pulsate. "Listen Davi. No disrespect but my brother Ali is not gay." "Listen my man it is a fucked up thing to hear but it is the truth." Davi pulled pictures out of the envelope and just like he said there was Ali kissing a man on the mouth as if it was women. I had seen him with the Spanish looking dude a couple of times. "Yo, can I use your bathroom." "Yeah the door next to the front entrance." I couldn't believe this shit. My own family, my brother, gay -- and putting our sister in this fucked up situation.

I felt the plate I had just eaten at the baby shower turning in my stomach. I had barely made it to the bathroom when I threw up everything I had just eaten an hour before. I washed my face with cold water. I had to get it together. This nigga was dead and that faggot ass nigga Ali was going to get his ass beat. Brother or not. Don't get me wrong I had nothing against gay men. But I did when it affected my family… and money.

I got myself together and went back to where Davi was waiting for me. "You good?" "Yeah I am good!" "Listen the shit is that this dude Pedro I know him." I looked at him puzzled. "Yeah, Yo! He sits at the table." This shit couldn't have gotten more fucked up and complicated.

This shit had me restless, Ali was gay. Then it all started coming back to me how he had little girlfriends but nobody to talk about. How he was extra when claiming pussy he had-- but turnd down many bad chicks. This dude's pillow talking placed my whole family in jeopardy.

This shit had me real fucked up. The worst part was the code in the street had Pedro in a guarded position. Everything in me made me question the code and make me want to body him anyway -- and face the consequences later.

When Davi said that Pedro sat at the table he meant that he was one of 10 men that handled business for the entire east coast, from Florida to Boston. They slung everything from smoke, ecstasy, any pill you could name, heroin, coke... you name it, they supplied it.

I had only heard about them growing up and they said no one really knew who they were except for their immediate family. The only way that you could fill one of those ten seats were if they were killed for dishonor or died of natural causes. I heard that they had everyone in their pockets from high ranking government officials to the lowly correctional officer.

Rumor had it that the current table is like the United Nations two ruthless Dominicans, two Russians, one Jamaican that would slice his own mother if she fucked with his money, two Puerto Ricans, one Asian, one Italian and an unknown that was at the head that no one talked about. I heard that at one time there had been a black man that was from Brooklyn from around my way but since then Brooklyn hadn't stepped up.

This shit had me fucked up. I was trying to get my mind right. I needed more information. I had been too fucked up to ask Davi any information so I had to put a plan together to find out who Pedro was and how I was going to deal with him. I hired my ghetto PI to follow Ali around hoping to find out a little more about his patterns and when he actually met with Pedro. So when I received the word I would put my game plan would be in place.

I was restless so I decided to call Davi and find out the status of this nigga's Pedro death date. "What up D?" "Chilling what's good?" "What's up with my man how is he doing?" "He is good for right now a little weak on his game so your boy might have to take his place and take his baby girl from him." "Oh yeah that's what's up? How long?" "Not much!" "Ok that's peace how about your family reunion." "That is still the same nothing has changed." "Good I will see you there tell your grand mom's I want some of that strong lemonade she makes" he laughed. "You got it."

I hung up, to the average person Davi and had just had a regular conversation. To a hustla that was hustling at it's finest. In that small conversation he had just informed me that Pedro would soon be ready to get his wig twisted back and that Davi would be replacing him at the table. I guess Pedro wasn't making the money he was supposed to and had been cutting corners so he would no longer be guarded by the table.

That was the best news I had heard all day. You see unlike niggas I was very patient and that is how I had survived in the game since the age of 14 and had managed to keep moving up in my position. Since Davi would soon be on the top me being his right man was bringing me a step closer to the table myself. His success made me successful.

During this same conversation Davi had also said that my reup was still on for this weekend and the reason why he laughed when I said strong lemonade was because I was making sure my product was on point. It made me feel a little better that shit was starting to look lovely it almost made me look forward to the birthday party Qahira was throwing for me in a couple of days.

When she originally told me about it I refused because I hate getting all that attention. So I told her fucking ass there was no way. So she did that ol' sucka shit and had my grandma's call me and tell me she was looking forward to going to my 25th birthday party and how at one time the way I was living she hadn't thought I would make it to this age. I chuckled "Come on Maw, was I that bad?" "Boy don't play me. You were worse!" I laughed "Maw where you getting that slang from?" "Boy you know Nico always talking that mess I guess I am catching on." Maw started laughing so hard she started coughing and wouldn't stop. "You ok Maw. Maw! Maw! Maw!" "Boy I am fine. Maw got to go but I will see you this weekend."

Since Maw brought Nico up I might as well go grab his punk ass. It was summer time so he was out of school. He was Qahira's son. She had him when she was 15. He was 12 now and feeling himself. He reminded me a lot of myself, real street smart. Damn. The only difference was he had Qahira to keep him focused on the books so he had the best of both worlds.

I decided to take the ride to Brooklyn instead of calling. Fuck it. If he wasn't there I would find some other shit to keep me occupied. It took me 25 minutes to make it to her house. I pulled up to Qahira's house and was pissed to find my faggot ass brother sitting on the stoop. I was tempted to drive away but he looked up before I could decide and waved to me.

"Qahira, Quron is here." "What up Ali?" I gave him the pound half ass and avoided looking him in the eye. I wasn't telling him nothing. I wanted to fuck his head up and make him understand how real the streets were when I put my plan in to place. Qahira hugged me, "what's up Q"? 'Nothing, How are you?" "Better, praise God!" "Where is Nico?" "You know him he is at the courts." "Good! That is exactly what I came to get him for." I walked up the block to the courts and watched my nephew playing ball with grown ass men. I smiled with pride. That's my boy. He was bringing it to the old heads. I sat and watched as one of my corner dudes started catching feelings about my nephew taking it to him.

It didn't help that one of his boys was talking shit. "Damn Yo! That little nigga is bringing it to you!" "Whatever nigga I don't see you out here." I continued to watch as Nico stripped the ball from dude and went up the court for the layup. "Damn Yo! Yah should double team him." "Damn nigga get off his dick!" Old boy was pissed since that was the game point.

My nephew walked off the court with the ball and started walking towards the door. "Young Dude!" He turned around, "what up?" "We aint done playing with the ball." "Listen OG, no disrespect but I am going home with my ball." "Maybe you didn't understand me we aint done playing with the ball." My nephew ignored him and continued to walk towards the opening. Corner boy tried to stop him and was found with a left hook from Nico.

I didn't want to step in yet since I wanted to make sure Nico could handle himself. The corner boy was dazed and looked at his people "You going to let this little nigga hit me?" "Nigga he about 12. We thought you could handle him yourself". Nico kept strolling out the opening and seen me watching the whole thing. "Unc, what up? You should of came earlier I would have shown you my skills."

At the same time the corner boys and his friends started after Nico to bank him. To his surprise corner boy looked up to see me. "Oh what up Q." "What up?" I didn't even know his name I just knew he was one of my workers. I watched as his people sat confused at what their next step should be. "Yo is this your people!" I looked at him like don't fuck with me, "my nephew". "Oh ok that's peace". I turned to Nico and said "let's get out of here". I turned around and seen the young dudes sitting there dumb faced. "Yo! A real nigga can take an ass whipping from a 12 year old." I heard a nigga say "I told you he was 12". "Fuck you nigga."

"Unc, so you did see my skills!" 'You awwiight!" "You know I could be that much better if I had some new kicks." "Real slick nephew! Didn't I just buy you some a week ago?" "Yeah but the new high-tops, baby blue and white just came out and you know I have to look fresh to death for the ladies." I laughed. "Boy what you know about the ladies?" "They be all over me. After all, I am a 5 10 sexy chocolate thing." "Boy I will see what I can do." I made sure that Nico always stayed fresh to death since his father wasn't in his life.

Since Nico had just came from the courts I decided to go the movies and see the new Will Smith joint that just came out. And fuck it, call me a softy-- I decided to cop him the new kicks he was talking about. I bought some clothes from the new boutiques near the mall for my birthday party. I also got every color fitted hat for my trip to Belize, a present to myself. I needed a break to get my mind right and some R and R.

JULISA SANTANA

I debated all week whether or not to go to sexy's birthday. I had been so programmed for so long. Since becoming a woman I had been Pito's woman, so I didn't even know how to even begin looking into the dating scene. I decided to go to the party anyways. I figured even if me and sexy didn't end up hooking up I would at least be able to mingle with other men besides the ones that worked for my father.

After asking almost all my friends to go the only one available was Cynthia and since she was the biggest Gold Digger of them all. She jumped at the opportunity of being surrounded by niggas with money. We drove Cynthia's car I didn't want to be the designated driver this time. I came to have fun.

The birthday party was at a very exclusive restaurant/club located in the Hamptons. It was one of those spots that unless you were a star or supplied drugs to the stars you wouldn't have access to even visit. So when I received the formal invitation on my email it made my decision to attend that much easier. The dress code was black and gold. According to Qahira those were Q's favorite colors. I wore a gold dress. It was cut low in both the front and the back , fitting snug and accentuating my hips and well toned ass. I completed the look with turquoise accessories. I must say I was looking and feeling good.

Cynthia was light skinned with hazel eyes, biracial, skinny and shaped like a supermodel. Guys loved to sport her because she was the Vanessa Williams type. Her only flaw was that she would cut anyone's throat for a couple of dollars. Tynese didn't fuck with her but I vouched for her on the note that she always kept it real and spotted a snake from miles away. She had tried to fuck with Davi before we became friends but he hadn't even given her time. He wasn't impressed. It was not a loss to her. She had many dudes lined up from athletes to tycoons of all races and religions.

We pulled up at the spot and I watched Cynthia's eyes sparkle like a kid at a candy shop. All the Maybachs with personal drivers, Maseratis, Benzs, Bmw and classic Cadillacs. This was definitely an official player's ball. We drove up to the valet parking and spotted some of the guests walking. There were new NBA draft picks, an anchor woman from the local TV station, a few people who just looked familiar. It made me think really who was this dude Q? Besides a good looking brother, what was he really about? In the back of my mind I knew I was only there to see him. There was something about him that intrigued me.

Cynthia and I walked into the ballroom to see a buffet of all the best cuisine, soul food and a nice ice sculpture of a crown. I liked his style the best food with a hood twist. We walked around and mingled with the guests, scoping to see who we might know. I spotted some guys that we knew worked for my pops and believe it or not some of Pito's friends were there. One had the nerve to ask if Pito knew I was there. I politely changed the subject and kept it moving. I finally saw Qahira and opted to stay close by hoping the guest of honor would be appearing soon.

Cynthia made her way to catch the attention of some dudes that where popping bottles. I played the wall and watched everybody having a good time. I felt someone watching me and turned around to see Trevor walking towards me. "Hi Julisa!" "Hi Trevor!" "What are you doing here?" "Oh! "He seemed surprised I had asked. "I am attending a function down the hall and seen you walking into the ballroom." This was starting to give me the creeps. I felt chills travel through my whole body and made a mental note to talk to Davi about this Trevor situation.

"So how have you been I have been missing you in class it seems like you are always rushing out?" "Yeah it's been a little crazy lately", since the whole Pito thing I hadn't even been able to enjoy classes the same. I was doing the bare minimum and just passing classes. I sat there awhile thinking of a way to get rid of Trevor without being disrespectful by saying nothing. "Well Trevor it was nice seeing you will you excuse me I have to go to the restroom." "Bye C-Chip."

I looked at him strangely. That was weird. Only my closest friends called me that. Davi had given me that nickname. He was five when I was born and when asked what he thought of the new baby he said, "she looks like a Chocolate Chip cookie" and it stuck. It was shortened to C-Chip. It had me a little worried how he had even known to call me by my nickname or felt that we had that comfort level. He smiled eerily and I kept it moving. I walked into the bathroom to see a group of the most glamorous women, one I thought I recognized from a Jay Z video.

"Girl I aint fucking with none of these big ballers. The dude I am trying to get at is that nigga Q. They say his pockets are deep. I got my fuck-em heels on and I know he is not going to be able to resist." "Girl that nigga fucked with my friend Spicy and she said that he has a big dick and knows how to work it. But you can forget about him wifeying anything. I heard he has never even has had a girlfriend and he is on some fuck them and leave them type shit."

"Girl he is so suspicious of chicks he's only using a condom he bought himself." "Girl that is cuz he aint never fucked with anyone like me. Bitches could stand in line because my dick sucking skills are legendary." They laughed to themselves. I was not trying to get caught up with a nigga that was in every bitch face. I decided to let Cynthia get her little time in and if she wasn't ready to go in the next half hour I would call my mother's driver to come get me.

I freshened up my lip gloss, washed and lotion my hands and headed out the door. As I headed out the door I tipped the attendant. I headed towards Qahira and grabbed my same spot against the wall. I watched the clock and headed to find Cynthia to let her know I was going to find a ride home.

I found her surrounded by what looked like a younger crowd eating up everything she said. "Excuse me" the crowd looked up to see who was disturbing Cynthia spotlight. "Damn Shorty let your friend join she is bad too. What's up Ms. Lady? How you doing? I looked around to see a young dude with gold fronts in his mouth with a white tee and the new Jordan's on his feet." He was real cute but not my style.

There was a time and a place to be street and classy and you could tell he was the type of dude that never knew nothing but street. "How you doing?" "Good now that you came." I smiled. "Cyn, I am going to catch a ride out of here. I will catch you tomorrow." "Girl, why you acting like that? You leaving so soon?" "Yeah girl!" I saw Cynthia's mouth drop as she looked past me. I turned around to see Q. "So you leaving baby girl?" I turned around and seen his pretty eyes and long eyelashes. Embarrassed, I looked down at his perfect white teeth.

"Well the guest of honor was taking so long I didn't think he would ever get here." He smiled, "well now I am here so now you have to stay". "Hello I am Cynthia, how are you doing?" I looked over "Sorry. Q this is my friend Cynthia. Cynthia, Q". Cynthia looked like she could have eaten Q alive. "How you doing?" He looked up at Cynthia and quickly looked into my eyes.

He grabbed my hand "so you can't even stay for me". "I am sorry baby I already called my ride so it's too late to cancel it." "Damn, so when am I am going to see you again." "Call me. You know the number?" "How about tomorrow?" "I don't know we will see" I smiled getting excited just thinking about seeing him again. My phone vibrated to alert me that the driver had arrived. That's my ride. I gave him a hug and waved to Cynthia and kept it moving.

Q's eyes followed me all the way to the front entrance. I turned back and waved. As I reached the front door, I saw Davi walking in. "What's up, CC? What are you doing here?" "Nah just came with my girl Cynthia but decided it was not my type of crowd so I am on my way out."

He looked at me puzzled! "Nina (little girl) don't get grown." "What are you talking about?" "Yeah ok, don't let me investigate." "Davi I am over 21. Get a life!" I laughed. I gave him a hug and kept it moving.

QURON JACKSON

I debated whether or not I should go after Julisa. Damn every time I was trying to get with her she was always escaping my clutch. "So baby, how come I have never met you before?" I turned around to see Julisa's friend Cynthia and felt her hand go around my waist. I smoothly grabbed her hand off kissed her hands and said "because we don't hang in the same crowds." "Oh yeah and what crowd is that." I smirked, "just different crowds." "Well sexy I would definitely like to hang with you sometime." I smiled, "baby girl I am really feeling your friend." "You sure, because it didn't seem like she was interested." "And plus baby girl you to skinny for my blood." I turned around and seen Davi chuckling at Cynthia's antics. "What up my dude? Thanks for coming." "No doubt!" "Cynthia, how you doing?" "Good Davi "she turned around towards the bar and went back into her groupie crowd.

"So let's talk business, do you want to head for the VIP?" "Damn dude do you ever rest today is your birthday we will have plenty of time to talk." "I smiled ok you got me but tomorrow I am meeting with you bright and early." He smiled, "alright".

The party was real nice. Qahira invited dudes I hadn't seen since elementary school. My cousins from the Atl and Bmore came through. Maw was even having a good time. The whole time I couldn't get my mind off ole girl even though some real proper chicks showed up to celebrate with the man. A lot of them definitely wanted to be my birthday present.

I left the party about 4 a.m. in the chauffeured limo Qahira had lined up. Waiting in the ride was this shorty I used to rock with Dyanna. She was cool. Real sweet girl studying to be an attorney. I figured I kept her around in case I ever got caught up in some dumb shit. "What's up Dyanna, what you doing in here?" "I was making sure you left with the only girl that really loves you." "Girl your crazy?" "For you baby!" I chuckled "so what you want me to do for you Q"? "Whatever comes to mind?" She sat there waiting on me to direct her. That was part of the problem she had been a good girl so long she didn't know how to take care of a nigga. She was definitely baby mother material but I couldn't make her my wife I would always be fucking around on her.

"Baby Girl come here come show daddy how much you love him." I unzipped my pants and directed her mouth down to my dick. Dyanna willingly began to suck on my dick like her life depended on it. "Yeah spit on it baby. Grab and squeeze the shit out of it while you sucking on that dick." She was getting excited just pleasing me. Dyanna was a real dark chocolate sexy chick from Nigeria. She was up here on a student visa. I met her at a gas station in Newark.

We had a frelationship (friendship and whenever I wanted to be bothered relationship). She was as close as I had ever gotten in a relationship. She had a sexy body built like where she was from straight from the mother land. Her family moved to England in her teenage years so she had a British accent. The best part about her that I fucked with was that she was naïve to the game and book smart as a fuck.

"Di come ride on this dick." She positioned herself on top and let me slide my dick slowly in her. Her pussy was so tight it felt like she was a virgin every time. Dyanna had no rhythm her lack of experience definitely showed I guided her up and down my hard stick and felt her moaning begin to increase. "I love you Q," damn I need to stop fucking with this girl. Hearing her say that made my dick almost go limp. Nah I'm fucking with you. When I felt her start to quiver and body go limp. I decided to get her excited again. I started sucking on her dark chocolate perky tities and stuck my finger in her ass while continuing to sway her on my stick up and down. I felt her begin to get excited again and like a boost of energy she started moaning again.

While continuing to satisfy her I rolled the window down to speak to the driver. To my pleasure it was a lady driver sexy blond with green eyes. "Can I help you sir?" While I continued to precede dicking Dyanna down I belted out Dyanna's address. There was no way she was coming to my house. That was definitely a no no. I watched as Blondie kept an eye the whole time on how I was making Dyanna feel and decided to keep the window down. The way Blondie was eye stalking we could have fucked around and had an accident.

I finished with Dyanna and walked her to her stairs she attempted to give me a kiss and I caught it with my cheek. Gave her a hug and kept it stepping. I got in the limo and gave the driver the address around the corner from my house. When we got a block from my crib Blondie said "sir you really seemed like you know what you were doing back there. You have enough in you for round two". I thought about it. Couldn't do it. She knew where I lived and I wasn't trying to get in no shit like that. "Give me a card. Maybe next time." Blondie handed me a card. I handed her a hundred and stood on a strangers stoop waiting for her to leave. Then I walked my happy go lucky ass to my house.

I woke up with a hang-over and still thinking about shorty. It was
1:00 p.m. so I decided to call her. "Jul, what up?" "Who is this?"
"Come on girl you got that many people calling you?" Jul knew
who it was but she didn't want to seem desperate and let Q know
no one else called her. Shit she had just gotten out of a forever
relationship she didn't even have game.

"Get ready I am coming to get you. Where you at?" "Boy I don't
know you like that. Why should I trust you." "Because I know
your brother." "I am at Fordham University." "Ok I will be there
in an hour." Damn small world. Dyanna my African shorty from
yesterday went to the same school but since she lived off dorm
and it was Saturday I wasn't worried about any problems plus she
knew we were just chilling so she couldn't catch feelings if she
spotted a nigga.

I decided to go with the Range since it drove smooth on the
highways and it had a lot of space for long trips. I was going to
make this a memorable first date for Jul. There was something
about this girl. Somewhere in the back of my mind I knew I had
to tell Davi about this whole sister situation. The thing was there
was no situation yet but I didn't want to disrespect a nigga and
push up on her without him knowing.

I decided to pack just my toothbrush and cologne and figured I
would purchase the other stuff I needed on the road. I arrived on
campus on time. I hated when mother fuckas made me wait.
Julisa was dressed in a pair of Capri's and an orange color wrap

around shirt with sexy sandals to match. She was sitting in front of the building when I arrived she was talking on her cell phone. I beeped to let her know I was there. She finished her conversation and jumped in my ride.

"So where are we going." "Why baby girl? You can't stay out all night?" She smiled "I am grown baby boy. Let's roll!" Jul put on her seatbelt and got comfortable in the leather seats. She seemed ok until she seen the 95 signs but tried to play it cool like she was down for whatever. I watched her and asked "are you ok?" "Yeah I'm good." "Why don't you pick out a CD so you can get comfortable. You seem a little nervous." She smiled and grabbed the CD case still playing cool. "Oh Q I have to put this in." She put in the CD and I waited to see what she liked. The sounds of Jaheim hit the speakers as we kept it moving on 95. I grabbed her hand and watched her start to relax and look out the window occasionally peeking my way.

"So what are you going to school for?" "I am working on an international business degree." "That's cool you plan on working for a big company when you graduate." "Nah my dad has businesses overseas and I hope to someday run them." She was doing big things. I liked that. "So what do you like to do or want to do?" "I want to travel. I haven't really had many opportunities to since my life revolved around going to jail cells. I'm sorry. I mean I would like to travel."

"Where do you want to go?" "I want to go to Hawaii, Egypt, and England all over!" "How about Belize?" "Yeah that would be hot." I made a mental note to go online and price how much it would be to have Jul join me on my trip. "So Q what is your deal? Do you work?" "Yes!" "What do you do?" "I have a construction business?" "Do you have a girlfriend?" "No!" "And why is that?" "Because I haven't met a good woman since my grandmother!" "Wow so your standards are pretty high?" "Yes, why settle for right now when you can get the real deal. I aint wasting my time on some chick just cause she looks good. She has to have something she brings to the table."

Q had just gotten one point. "So what do you like to do?" "I enjoy sports going to Boxing matches, traveling, watching the game or just chilling at home." "What would you like to do that you have never done?" He looked at me seriously. "Don't laugh, I would like to go skiing." Jul laughed. "Damn girl didn't I tell you don't laugh." He looked serious. "Nah baby that's cool I love skiing it is tiring but its real cool."

"Have you ever been to Baltimore?" "No!" "Well now you will be able to say you traveled somewhere?" Jul face was shocked but she kept quiet and played it off extra cool. We were quiet for the next half hour until the CD stopped for Jul's next selection. Jagged Edge, Stevie Wonder and Maxwell played on the stereo as our conversation flowed and we got to know each other. She was real cool and the more I knew about her the more I was feeling this girl.

JULISA SANTANA

We pulled up to see a Harbor and I couldn't help but feel like a little girl. I saw the boats and people walking around, street entertainers and people just relaxing getting sun. Baltimore reminded me of a small New York. We got on a water taxi. It was crazy. A boat that actually worked as a cab and ended up dropping us off directly in front of a nice restaurant. I was impressed and excited. I had to get my nerves right so as soon as we were seated I excused myself to the restroom so that I could get some coke in my system. I wasn't an addict. I just used when my nerves were on edge.

"Q excuse me, I have to go to the bathroom." "That's funny me too." I followed Jul and watched as her ass jiggled in her Capri's I watched her calves they look like they were smooth as butter I would love to have them wrapped around any part of me I smiled.

I walked with a little switch because I knew Q was watching. "I'm going to meet you right here." I walked in the ladies bathroom and heard some noise. I looked under the stall to find four feet a ladies high heels and a dudes timberland boots. I heard slurping which got me a little excited. I walked two steps back and back out the door and knocked on the men's room door and peeked and yelled Q's name. "Q, Q, are you in here" just as I stepped in I seen Q at the urinal he turned around and my eyes went down to his dick he had the biggest thickest black dick I had ever seen. Instantly I felt my pussy start pulsating and felt my panties get moist. I stayed focused on his member licked my lips and pictured how good his dick would feel inside my pussy. "Jul, Jul!" I looked up embarrassed as he smirked. "You good?" "Oh yeah I need to use this bathroom can you look out for me." "No doubt!" I went into the stall. "You need help?" I laughed. "Yeah right. Maybe another time."

I came out the bathroom and looked over at Q checking his cell phone and posted up against the wall. Damn he was sexy, chocolate, 6' 1 and a nice ass body. I looked up at his lips and wanted to kiss him. I washed my hands, grabbed a paper towel and started walking towards the door and all I could think about was fucking him. I would make sure he wouldn't even think about any other pussy but mine. I would suck his dick like my life depended on it.

He must have felt something was going on because as soon as we walked out the door he turned me around and said, "Jul I am glad you came out with me." He gave me a hug and I smelled his cologne. It was so sexy. I felt my nipples get excited as I felt his upper chest. It felt like he definitely took care of his body. He put his lips on my neck and they felt soft. I felt my pussy and panties just getting wetter and wetter.

He looked into my eyes and gave me a soft kiss I grabbed his lips and slowly sucked on his bottom lip. He stood back and licked his lips and said, "I like that. Does that mean we ready to go?" I just looked at him and didn't say anything.

I followed Q back to the table, and sat down we were both quiet for a moment until the waiter came up and asked for our order.

When the waiter left Q finally said "nah baby girl we aint taking that route just yet. We have plenty of time. Plus I want you to respect me in the morning." I laughed. "Ok".

The rest of the night was real nice. We had caricatures drawn, he bought me a rose from the vendor but finally when it got dark we decided to head home. We had a 2 ½ hour drive home so we decided to make it an early night. As we reached close to the city I hesitated to ask Jules to come to the house. I was trying to be real good. I wanted to speak with Davi before I had made any moves. Plus I didn't want to scare her off. But I was having such a good time I didn't want to end the night just yet. "So do you want to come home with me we can watch a movie." I watched her as she debated the good girl in her wanting to say no but the grown woman in her saying yes.

We both stayed silent as we headed to his house. I think we were both afraid to fuck up the mood. It seemed like the drive had taken forever as I watched Q zig zag through streets and going around in circles and finally get to his house. We approached a beautiful gated community. Which made me start to understand why Q was so confident? It showed in his walk, his presence it even showed when he walked in a room. I knew about dudes like Q. Being that my father was in the game I had met a lot of men that looked the part fresh to death, cars and really shiny but eventually expired.

Q seemed very calculated like he was going to be around for the long haul. Real thorough yet keeping it sexy. You could put him in any type of environment and he could fit right in. That was just how I was and I liked that. As we drove into his u-shaped driveway I looked up to see a huge colonial style, red brick house.

I stopped before we walked into the front door. I stopped Q before we walked in his door, "Listen it has been 3 years". He grabbed my chin and looked into my eyes "Baby girl we are chilling. There is no rush".

As we walked in I was amazed at how his home was decorated. It had an elegant, classic appeal with a modern touch. "Baby do you want to see a movie?" "What do you have?" "Let's go see!" We walked down a flight of stairs into a circular hallway where we were surrounded by doors. "You want popcorn?" I nodded. He grabbed the door that was directly straight ahead, that lead into a movie theatre. On our way in Q started the old fashioned popcorn machine. Make yourself at home "Mi Casa es Su Casa" (My House is Your House). "Ok Q, let me find out you know a little Spanish." He laughed only a little. "I will be right back."

I looked around and started feeling real glamorous. My family was doing well but Q was young and already wanting for nothing. I looked in the movie case and found my favorite movie "Brave Heart". Went to the projector and tried to figure out how to open it. Q walked in with jogging pants on and a wife beater. In his hands he had a t-shirt, shorts and two water bottles. He handed me the short and t-shirt, here slip into something more comfortable. I gave him the movie and stood there looking at him. "My bad. I feel so comfortable like you been here before. It's the first door on your right."

Damn believe it or not I was nervous as hell I felt like this was my first date ever. I brought Jul down some shorts and a t-shirt but all I wanted was for her to get naked so I could lay her down and look at every inch of her body naked. I looked down at the movie she picked. No shit! One of my all time favorite movies besides "Scarface".

I was so happy that Jul had agreed to come home with me I didn't say nothing to her the whole ride. Then I had to do my regular routine to make sure no niggas was following me. I didn't want to rush Jul especially after all that nigga had put her through. Since my birthday and getting to know her all I wanted to do was be in her face and take care of her. I heard the popcorn machine stop and went to the cabinet to grab butter, salt and anything else she needed.

When I first built this theatre I had debated about getting the movie seats. Now I am glad I got the recliners that sit two. I sat down in the front and waited for Jul to come out the bathroom.

I came out with just Q's t-shirt since the shorts were entirely too big and kept falling down. The T-Shirt was big enough of to cover my entire body. "Here you go." "Real cute, what size are these shorts XXXL?" "Nah," he Laughed. "Baby girl come on sit next to me." I sat and felt the warmth of his body on my left side. What was I thinking? We hadn't done shit and I was already excited? If I wasn't so nervous I would have straddled him and put his ass to sleep.

The movie started and I felt his arm go around me and smell my hair. About 25 minutes into the movie I heard Q's rhythmic breathing I turned around and looked over at him sleeping. God he was even sexy sleeping. I kissed his lips. He opened his eyes and just looked at me. His eyes pierced through me making my pussy jump. He grabbed my face and started kissing me softly on the forehead, eyes, lips and neck. I let out a moan that sent chills down my back. He pulled off my t-shirt to reveal my black lace panty set. He released my left breast from the bra and softly bit on my nipple.

He put his soft lips on the tip and sucked on it like it was a piece of candy. I felt my pussy walls starting to get wet and grabbed his head so he could devour me. He continued to suck on my breast and pulled my panties to the side and slipped his finger inside of me. I felt my neck jerk back and raised my ass so he could make me feel good. He massaged my clit softly and flicked it gently. He slid his fingers in and out to the movement of my hips. I licked his lips and swallowed his tongue and started sucking on it like it was a dick. He continued to softly pump his fingers in and out as my juices drenched his hand. I looked down to see his pants and seen his long thick stick screaming to come out.

I grabbed it and let it free. It was so thick and long I couldn't wait to feel it fill me. I was really nervous even though I wasn't a virgin I had only been with Pito and his was half Q's size. I licked my hand for lubrication and started jerking on his dick. I was jerking it so hard I swear he is going to scream. Instead he said squeeze the shit out of that dick baby girl, harder. I felt myself about to come excited by his hands, mouth and just seeing how big his dick is. My body shook and I felt my body release cumming loudly I moaned AAAHH we both start laughing. I blushed embarrassed.

"I guess it has been 3 years. Baby girl you ready for this.?" I knew quite well I couldn't stop but I was trying to be a gentleman. "I am going to grab a condom because I don't want you to be my baby mama --at least not yet. Maybe my wife first, and then mother of my children second." I placed the condom on and thought about how moist and warm that pussy would be. I grabbed her by the waist and made her straddle me. I slipped her panties to the side and slowly placed my dick near her pussy and popped her clit with my dick.

"You sure you want this?" "Q stop playing let's do this." I slowly slid my dick half way in because it was so tight. "Hmmm it feels so good Papi." I grabbed her ass and slowly slid her ass onto my dick in a grinding motion. "Oh baby it feels so good. Q it feels so good." She grabbed me and started inching it slowly all the way down. "I love this dick Q. It feels so good in my pussy." She had me so excited I wanted to cum right then but I didn't want her to think I couldn't last. I stopped moving. "Baby what happened", Jul said. "You weren't acting like you wanted any."

She looked at me with sexy eyes and said "so you want to play games? Ok". She got up and turned around and started riding me backwards. She started slowly, moving up and down as I watched her fat ass popping up and down on my dick. Her clit grazing my balls. Damn this had to be the best pussy I ever had. I felt her stop midway and get up. "What's the problem Q?" "Who is playing games now?" I laughed, "Get your pretty ass over here". I placed her back on my dick and pushed her all the way down as I felt her nails dig my thighs.

"You can handle this." " AAAAHHH Papi Conyo que bueno (Damn, how good this feels)." I watched her long black hair bouncing up and down on her round ass, her juices dripping on my hairs. I grabbed her hips and started pushing as far as I could go. I wanted to put my whole body inside of her if it fit. I heard her moaning as I wiggled my dick as far as it could go every time she came down on it. I grabbed her clit and started swaying her ass and started feeling her movement getting faster. I licked my finger to make her clit even wetter and felt her body jerk and legs start shaking as I felt her warm cum through the condom which instantly made me cum.

She fell exhausted on my body and seemed drained from all the excitement. I picked her up and carried her to my bathroom where I began to bathe her sensually. Damn I was excited again as I watched her. "Q that was so good" she said through a yawn. I rinsed her off and walked her to the room and laid her on the bed. She was sleeping before I even had a chance to get out the shower. I went downstairs to watch the ESPN highlights and called Qahira. "Hira, your brother is in love." "With who boy?" "Spanish shorty, I just met." "Really are you going to tell your boy you sleeping with his sister?" I thought about it! "I will have to ask her what she wants to do." "Well don't get in any problems secrets eventually come to surface." "I know, I know." Damn. Yet another thing on my plate.

"Q!" "Yes baby." "I hear someone downstairs." "That is Sophia my cook/cleaning lady it's alright." "Boy let me find out you so lazy you got a chef." "Nah it's just that if I don't I will always be eating out, so she helps me." Jul got up and slipped on her clothes and went down stairs. I went back to sleep damn it felt good to have a woman in the house. It was Saturday and if it was up to me Jul and I would have stayed in the bed all weekend.

I woke up two hours later to find Sophia and Jul talking like they had been friends for years. It was cool I never brought any woman to my house so there was nothing fucked up she could say about me. Plus Sophia had been working for me for about 3 years and she was family. I smiled.

"What's up sleepy head? You finally getting up?" Yeah, I gave her a hug and whispered in her ear "you put me to bed". She smiled. Sophia walked out of the room quietly leaving us alone to snuggle. "So what's the plan for the day?" "I don't know. You feel like dropping me off at the dorm." "Nah I want you to stay with me." Jul laughed. "Me too baby, but I don't have any clothes." "No problem lets hit the stores and go to a movie or something." "Ok sugar daddy." I laughed. She didn't even know I was ready to spend everything I had on her. I had no limits. It wasn't the sex. It was everything.

The past couple of weeks were crazy. A month passed and I was really feeling Jul. She had stayed at my house since the day we had made love and the only days she had went home was the days she had class. We couldn't get enough of each other. I had never understood how people fell in love and got so caught up that they could die for someone else. My life had been real hard and the only women I had loved where in my family.

I watched Jul's naked body in the moonlight as she lay between my legs. She looked like the color of copper and her long hair lay wet on her back. This was not the time to fall in love. I was at war and if my enemies were as smart as I was any weakness would be the way to defeat any opponent. "Baby you sleeping." "Nah." "I can't believe how fast we are moving this feels crazy. I am waiting for something bad to happen. This past month has felt like years."

I just listened. I loved just hearing her raspy voice. "Q don't hurt me." I couldn't let her know that I was so caught up she could really hurt me. This was new to me, unknown territory. "Come on baby this relationship will have to be built on trust and respect. I will never do anything intentionally to hurt you. "

I needed Jul in my life and didn't know what I had ever done without her. She made me feel inspired like this game wasn't the only thing I could love and count on. "Baby if I ask you to do something silly will you do it for me." "Yeah as long as it aint no gay shit." "Come on seriously. Will you pray with me?" She caught me by surprise just when I thought I might not be able to care about this woman anymore she made me feel even more crazy.

"I haven't prayed since I was 13 years old. I don't think God wants to hear from me." "Of course he does Q. He forgives everything we do." "Nah not some of the shit I have done." "Please Q, ok repeat after me Our father who art in heaven, hollow be thy name thy kingdom come thy will be done on Earth as it is in Heaven give us this day our daily bread and forgive us as we forgive those who trespass against us and lead us not into temptation and deliver us from evil. Amen. God will you keep our families safe and keep our relationship in your hands. God we ask that you guide our path and don't allow the devil to come into our hearts and our lives Amen." I knew right then that this woman would be my wife.

I lay with Q and wondered why I had lasted so long with Pito how God had brought us both into each other's path when we most needed each other. I think in the back of my heart even though I was with Pito I knew he was not my soul mate but sometimes it's hard to see that when that is all you know. I didn't even know if lying with Q made me want to cry, scream or what. This past month I waited for something to go wrong. What was he hiding where were the other women? Was he a woman beater or everything under the sun? Since the first night we spent together the only time we had been apart was if I had to go to school or for Q to handle his business. I used to wonder if you could love a person as much as they love you? Was that even possible?

Growing up I would see that Mami loved Papi so much more than he could ever love her. I vowed never to be like that. Don't get me wrong Papi never hurt Mami physically and she wanted for nothing. But I think her hurt was worse. It was emotionally. We all heard about the other women and we were kids so I can imagine all the things Mami heard. She dealt with his indiscretions all the time.

"Baby you ok." "Yeah I am good so what are you trying to get into today. Today is my grandmother's birthday and I want you to come with me so she can meet my future wife." "Ok Q save it we have only been together for a month, so don't swell my head up."

"I am serious Jul." "Yeah, ok." Q looked around the room I am going to prove it to you. "What are you looking for?" He grabbed money out of his pocket and pulled the two black rubber bands that were holding his money together. "Come on we are about to have a private ceremony." "Stop Q my family doesn't even know about us." "Who's fault is that?" "I know, I know but it's so soon after Pito I don't want them to feel like I am rushing things." "Well then this is about us." He grabbed my hand.

"I Q, the baddest, flyest looking Nigga to come out of Brooklyn if I

LOVE, SEX & THE HUSTLE

say so myself take the sexiest, smartest, nastiest in a good way Jul Milagros Santana to be my wife." I laughed "boy you are crazy". He slid the black rubber band on my ring finger. Baby this represents us being committed loving each other and married in our eyes. Just as he handed me the other rubber band it popped. I got you girl we will never run out of these.

I grabbed it and laughed "Quron Malik Jackson if we do take vows I expect a nice ring even if we don't have a ceremony". " I got you baby." "Quron, you will be faithful, and you will never let me down intentionally and you will never do anything to hurt me." I slipped the rubber band on his ring finger. "Wait that aint right you are supposed to tell me what you will do for me." I slipped off my robe "I promise to fuck you, suck you, make love to you, massage you and love you as long as we both shall live." "OOOhh I like that. I think this calls for honeymoon time. Ding Ding here goes Round Three." "Boy we just got out the bed." "So it will be that much faster for us to get back in."

JULISA SANTANA

"Girl, where have you been? I am surprised you had time to meet with me for lunch." "What are you talking about? I talk to you almost every day?" "Yeah but I haven't seen you since we came from the Doctors office." "I know Ty I have been caught up." "Yeah I heard Cynthia told me the low down and I heard the brother is fine and he and his people are doing it. You are so wrong Jul. I haven't even had an opportunity to meet him. Damn is it that serious?"

"He is so good to me but you know that is how they all start. That is what I thought about Pito and look where that landed me. I am so scared Ty." "Why? Don't let Pito tear up your hope just because he wasn't for you. There are good men out here you better be lucky that you snatched him up before some other chick put her claws on him. According to Cynthia if he would have met her first that would have been her man."

"No Ty she didn't". "Yes girl keep her away from Q, you remember what she did to Ebony, she was all in her face finding out all about Bibo and stuff then she end up fucking him in her own house."

"Ty you are bugging she was young then and she ended up being with him for 3 years." "Yeah that's because Bibo knew her style and was scared to let her go outside so would stay beating her ass. He still would be if he didn't end up getting Fed time."

"Girl you are crazy, so how is my god daughter." "She is fine, girl I do not need another women in my house. Momma, Tiasha and I are quite enough." "So how are your baby daddies?" "Girl that is another story it has been a constant headache. Black is determined that this baby is his because he said Julio is too pussy to make any babies. And Julio is pressuring me to get married telling me to think about the baby and how his health insurance is better than mine. How this is going to be his parents first grandchild. Girl he is already picking out names."

"No Ty." "It gets worse. I am at the grocery store with Black and I see Julio's mom and she is steady asking me about how I am feeling. How I need to eat right and all and Black the whole time is giving her the dirtiest looks and I swear he is about to blow up but he doesn't say anything the whole time. I just knew he wouldn't have said anything out of respect but girl I almost peed on myself right then." "Ha, Ha, Ha you are crazy, girl."

"So what are you going to do when the baby is born?" "I don't know I am trying to get over my first visit and who I should invite. It's going to be a long 5 more months." "Girl I swear you stay with drama." "Hello Ladies are you ready to order?" "Yes, can I have the special?" "And I will have the Steak and Shrimp with a baked potato." "Ty let me find out you are going to blow up." "I don't know I might," she laughed. Ty never weighed more than 110 pounds growing up and now that she was pregnant she probably had gained 5 pounds if that.

It was great seeing Ty and catching up. I hadn't realized how much time I had been spending with Q until I seen her little belly growing reminding me of how long I had been away from my friend.

"Mi Nina (my baby girl) how you doing?" I felt chills run down my spine as I heard Pito's voice. Ty's mouth dropped. "Tynese, how you doing?" "I am good Pito? How you doing?" They hugged. It had been three years. "So you're not going to get up and say hi to an old friend? No hug no nothing." I got up hesitantly and hugged Pito in a trance. It took 5 seconds for us to separate as I felt tears run down my eyes knowing that my past was once this man.

I quickly wiped my tears as I seen his mom and sister walk in. "Hey Jul, how are you doing?" "I am good Tia (auntie)," I gave Pito's mom a hug. "How is everything?" "Good, we are here celebrating Pito's release why don't you join us?" "No, Ma his sister chimed in. She already has company?" "Lisa, Jul is family we can catch up?" "Actually Tia we were just leaving." Thank God right at that time the waiter came with the check with great timing. Ty got up getting the hint. Pito's mom said good bye and his sister just looked at me like she had beef. Shit I didn't do anything to her, her brother was the fucked up one.

"Can I speak to you for a minute?" I looked at Ty. She gave me a go ahead look. We walk into the lobby of the restaurant and sat in the waiting area. "Listen, I just want to tell you that I am sorry, about how everything went down." "How could you betray us like that?" "Mi Nina (My baby girl) it wasn't about us it was about my freedom. Do you understand that? I love you, you are supposed to be my wife, and you will be my wife."

"Pito I have moved on." "Yeah the streets are talking I heard some dude from Brooklyn. I know you Jul you aint given my love to no one else. We gonna get over this." "It is too late, I am feeling him." Pito's ears were finally registering what I was saying and somewhere deep down he knew I had given Q his love. "Julisa! Julisa!" I watched as the vein on his head started bulging and felt his grip get tighter. "That dude does not want problems; this is a war he can't win." "Damn Pito after three years you have not changed. I have to go."

"I will call you. This conversation is not over." I walked back to Ty who was crunching ice chips waiting patiently. "You ok?" "Yeah girl long story, let's go." This was so wrong I felt stuck between my past and present. The man I had loved for so long and the man I felt would be my husband.

QURON JACKSON

I heard the faint sound of my cell phone as I tried to get up fast enough to pick it up. Who was calling me at 5:00 a.m. "Yo!" "Q!" "Yeah!" "Get ready!" With that the phone went dead. My body instantly got up as I went downstairs to my gym and felt my body getting tight and my mind getting right. The time had come this dumb ass nigga was finally going to pay and I had been getting ready for a minute this nigga Pedro would feel the same wrath his wife had met and Ali's bones would finally get kicked the fuck out of the closet. Since I really didn't trust motha fuckas and my brother was involved I decided to handle this myself. Plus it was personal I needed to make Ali understand that this life and the streets were real and fucked up.

It was early morning around the time that everybody was trying to get to work the best time to catch a nigga slippin. I had called Ali the night before told him I wanted to take him to this new spot for breakfast so to be ready in the a.m. He was with it even though it had been a while since I had even done anything with the nigga we was still brothas.

We pulled up to the train station and I looked over to see Ali's face look suspicious and he seemed uneasy. But I played it cool I was determined to finish what was about to pop off. Ali's face turned from worry to fear, he looked like he could have shitted on himself as we pulled up on the train Pedro took every day.

Ali finally got enough nerve to speak. "Q, why are we here?" Stone faced, I replied "I have to take care of some business. Walk with me." As we walked through the aisles of the train station we saw Pedro standing at the end. Without Ali noticing I quickly separated myself from him. Pedro looked up and saw Ali and starting smiling and waving for him. I was so far ahead of Ali he didn't see that I had grabbed my nine and put the silencer on. Pedro started walking towards my brother showing him love, right then the train arrived.

I pulled up my piece and shot Pedro in the head. I watched him fall down as blood splattered on my brother's face. Shock and tears filled Ali's eyes. Before he could react I pushed Pedro's body on the tracks. In shock my brother sat there stunned, I grabbed my shit and hit him in the back of his head. In a stupor I dragged him like a drunk up the escalator stairs. As we hit the platform I heard screams as people had finally seen Pedro's body. At that point all hell broke loose making it that much easier to get out unnoticed. I threw Ali in the backseat and headed to the spot.

JULISA SANTANA

Since the restaurant ordeal Pito had been blowing up my phone but I had too much to deal with and everything in my body was telling me to avoid him. Q and I were doing real well so much it was actually scary. We had even met his family in an intimate get together his people threw for his grandmother for her birthday. They seemed real close except for his brother in law who seemed to rub me the wrong way. My family was starting to suspect me and Pito weren't together anymore and Davi had almost caught Q and I together at some of the local hang out spots.

It was Thursday night which meant my family got together at Caruso's to eat and hangout. It was the only time we had time for each other. As long as I could remember we have been going there. I didn't plan on staying long I was hoping to meet with Q after dinner. When I got to the restaurant I looked in the parking lot and seen that Mami and Papi had both arrived. They always drove in separate cars for safety purposes. The only car missing was Davi's. I pulled up next to a dark tinted Cadillac that looked familiar and headed towards the door of the restaurant.

As I grabbed the door I felt a hand touch mine at the handle. I turned around to see none other than Pito. My heart skipped a beat. I couldn't lie he was looking real sexy. He had on a nice pair of jeans with a white T and blazer and Prada's to match. "What are you doing here?" "You didn't think I was going to miss the family dinner did you?" "I don't think you should be here." I seen the vein on Pito's head pop out he was pissed. "Julisa!" Oh shit he was using my government he was mad. "Who should be here that nigga? Get the fuck out of here! That nigga aint got the years we have invested!" "Listen this aint the time or place." "Pito!" I turned around to see Papi. "How you doing?" "I'm good now Mr. Santana." "Why haven't we seen you since you have been home?" "Sorry. No disrespect. Just trying to be on the grind. Julisa and I were just about to walk in." I rolled my eyes just enough for Pito to catch it as he opened the door wider to let me in before him. He grabbed the small of my back and I felt the heat rise through my body as he directed me into the door.

Pop, Pop, Pop, Pop noise that sounded like fireworks exploded around me as I heard glass shatter. Pito pushed me to the ground with force making me land on my handbag stabbing me with my own car key. I heard Papi say; "is everybody alright" I turned around to see my father grabbing his side and watched as blood was turning his once cream shirt to dark pink. "Papi, are you ok?" "Yeah it's just glass. Where the fuck is security? Why am I paying you muthafuckas?"

They all rushed to my father too late. My father was furious. "Dino, Jose take my wife and mother home. Chulo get me David on the phone. Where the fuck is he? Pito take my daughter home and if anything happens to her its your ass. She is to stay with you tonight no matter what she says." Pito smirked and looked at me as my mouth dropped. "I will get your car home. Ride with Pito." "But Papi!" "But nothing!" We were all escorted out the back as Papi started making calls this wasn't the first time they had attempted to kill my father but it was the first time his family had gotten involved.

I sat in silence in Pito's car as we headed who knows where. I was so upset. I didn't know what to do. I had to tell Q what was going on without involving him with family business. I knew Pito would not just have me calling another dude whether we were together or not. I wanted to text Q and let him know I would see him tomorrow and that I was ok. I fished in to my pocketbook for my blackberry and went to text him when I seen my screen was cracked damn my phone had broken. It must have been when I landed on it. Damn could my night get any worse?

"Mi Niña (my baby girl) I have to make a stop but then we heading straight home." We pulled up to the Caribbean spot and Pito got out. I know this motha fucka was not leaving me outside the spot so he could cop some smoke. This was some bullshit. About 15 minutes later he came out with two big brown bags. I smelled his cologne and curry chicken which at one time was two of my favorite things. "I got you chicken. Is that ok?" "Yeah", I sat back to relax. There was no need to make this worse. I might as well go with the flow or it was going to be a long night.

I sat back listening to Jagged Edge thinking about Pito and I, Q and I and what I really wanted in my life. I turned towards the window as I felt tears run down my eyes. Pito had fucked up. I was moving on. I played with my black rubber band engagement ring feeling helpless stuck between the life I was trying to make and the life I had always had.

Pito was now staying in the condominiums that had just been built in a nicer area of New Jersey. It was real nice as always, real clean and the finest of things in his crib. "Jules let me show you something." He brought me into his bedroom and there was a sketched poster size picture of me and him on his wall that fit with the black and white color scheme of his bedroom set."

"That is nice but what will your baby mama say!" "Come on Jules it was a fucked up situation. You didn't even let me explain. They had me stuck. It was either get caught up on another case or fuck with Shorty. What was I supposed to do?" "Pito we were supposed to have babies, we were supposed to be together I gave you my whole teenage years. Here it is I am a grown woman and never even knew what it was to be with another man. I knew all the shit you had done in the past even when you thought I didn't. You are having a baby! That doesn't go away."

"Mi Niña (baby girl)! I love you baby girl. I aint ever loved any other woman but you. So what our paths got crooked? We can make them straight. Come here." I was fucked up Pito grabbed me from behind and started kissing my neck. My head was turning. Pito was slowly taking off my shirt and rubbing my pussy over my pants. He knew my body and what felt good. I was completely naked except for my heels. Pito walked around me to admire my body.

He grabbed his penis and slowly started kicking off his shoes and pants. He had on the sexy briefs I liked on him. He took off his shirt to reveal a new tattoo I had never seen. I tried to look but at that moment he grabbed me and laid me on the bed. He grabbed my calves and massaged them sniffing my body like he couldn't get enough of my scent. He turned me around and smacked my ass rubbing his nose up the back of my leg all the way up my back. He bit my mole on my right ass cheek. I heard him whispering "estoy es mio (this is mine)". He flipped me around and nibbled slowly on my inner thigh and spread my lips open as a moan escaped my body. Damn it was true what they said about Dominicans. They sure can eat pussy.

My body was in convulsions by the time Pito got up. My body was drained from having had multiple orgasms. I felt Pito slide inside of me and started kissing me passionately like he couldn't get enough of me. He was in a trance. "Julisa I will kill that dude. This is my pussy." My mind was stuck between loving Q and Pito and the feeling that my body was feeling right now. After what it seemed like hours, Pito finally came and I was drained from all the excitement of the shooting that night and this love triangle I was creating. I fell fast asleep.

Hours later I woke up to hear Pito slightly snoring and a feeling of shame came over me as I got out of the bed. It had to be about 3am I quietly grabbed all my stuff and looked around for mail to find out Pito's address so I could call a cab. I ran out the door pushed the door closed and waited outside so they wouldn't beep the horn waking Pito up. The whole ride home I thought about my situation I needed time away from both of them it was too much. I contemplated calling Q letting him know I was ok but instead decided to get rest and think about what my game plan was and who I wanted to be with.

QURON JACKSON

In my plan I knew that I had to let Ali know that this was a fucked up game and let him feel the pain he could have caused our whole family. Instead I was contemplating where I wanted to go with this as let him sit at the spot tied up wondering what the fuck had gone wrong. I decided to go to my old stomping grounds and grab a drink at this little lounge to get my mind right. I had been calling Jul all day with no answer not even a text to let me know she was alright. I needed her right now to at least to get some of this shit out of my mind.

The spot was a mixed older crowd you could find senators, mayors drug dealers anybody that had money and needed a place to have privacy there. If you didn't want people in your face it was the place to go. I usually didn't sit at the bar but I was feeling like that tonight. Fuck it I would shoot the shit with the bartender and watch the game. I sat and looked around to the scope scene. There were a couple of ladies at the end the bar. One looked familiar but I dismissed it and ordered my drink.

The Knicks were losing by 10 damn. "How you doing baby?" I turned around to see Jul's grimy friend, which I knew was trying to fuck a nigga. She was thirsty but she was definitely a cutie. "I'm good baby girl how you?" "Just relaxing you mind if I sit." "No Problem, what you drinking?" "Gran Marnier, wow that is how you do?" "Not too many people know about that." "Hey, have you spoken to Jul's today?" I wanted Shorty to know Juls was still on mine and let her know she wasn't fucking with my girl. "Baby I am the wrong person to ask that shit because I am a real bitch and I don't hold my tongue for nobody."

What was she getting at? "Let's talk about something sexier like me and you?" "Come on baby girl you know I am with your girl." "Wow you real loyal to a chick that aint thinking about you." "What you mean?" "Sexy she is with her old man I guess she figure she could juggle both of you." I knew shorty was fucked up but something told me she wasn't lying. Even though she was cruddy she knew I could go to the source. I sat there stunned not knowing if I should be mad or feel stupid for falling for a woman for the first and last time.

I wanted Jul's to hurt like I did and sat there festering. After 3 shots my anger had taken over any sense I had. This was fucked up. I never let emotions take over but this had me really going crazy. I finally turned to look at the source of my anger and the only one that could pay right now for Jul's indiscretion.

"Baby you ready to go?" I looked at her and for one second thought twice. Fuck it if she wanted to feel the dick she was going to feel it. Do you mind if my girl goes too. I turned around to see a skinny ebony model type chick? The more the merrier.

Even though a nigga heart was fucked up, my dick wasn't. So I turned to Shorty and was like "let's head out". She whispered in her girl's ear and popped her on the ass. We all got up and started walking out the door. I bought a bottle of Henny before we walked out the door; it was going to be a long night. We got on the elevator to the parking garage. Cynthia pushed her friend against the elevator wall and lifted her skirt as I watched. She slid her red thong down her legs that looked like smooth cocoa. She turned her around to show me her ass and I seen her pussy peaking out from underneath. Cynthia lifted one of her legs showing her calves and silver stiletto heels cocked up on the rail of the elevator. Cynthia sucked her two fingers and slid them in to chocolate's pussy and began grinding them in and out and with her other hand she grabbed my erect dick and began to jerk it slowly. Her friend looked into my eyes and softly purred. I grabbed her nipple through the material of the dress.

The ding of the elevator got us back into the motion. We decided to ride in my car. On the way to the telly I was feeling fucked up about Jul so I called her one last time. Her phone went right to voicemail. My pride and dick had me fucked up. There was no turning back. Here I am trying to marry Shorty and she was with her ex.

JULISA SANTANA

The next morning I decided to go and get a new cell phone. Just as Daddy had promised my car was sitting outside my dorm. While at the mall I decided to change my cell phone number. Fuck it I needed space and needed to figure out what to do about the Q and Pito thing and being in touch with them was not going to help matters. I drove to my parents house to sleep in my own room and get my thoughts right.

Since it was Sunday our housekeeper was off and as usual my mother was cooking breakfast. "Mamita, what is wrong with you? Are you and Pito ok?" Tears instantly ran down my eyes, "no mom we are not alright, we are not together anymore". "What do you mean? But you were all good last night." At that moment my father walked in, "what is going on?" "Nothing Papi!" "Now there are no secrets in this family first David is nowhere to be found. Now this shit. I can't take to much more." He sat down like he was going to have a heart attack.

I sat down. I had never lied to him before so I was not going to start now. "Papi, Pito and I are no longer together I have met someone new." "Since when? What is going on? I told him what had happened with Pito and the baby." My father sat silent his eyes went into a deadly slant. "I'm sorry, so who is this new guy." "He is a friend of Davi but Davi doesn't even know about us." "What is his name?" "Q, Papi!" My father's mouth dropped, "small fucking world".

"Mr. Santana, oh shit." Chulo came into the room with a gun to his head Davi behind him. "What is going on Davi, Mami screamed?" "Ask your fucking husband?" My father's face went grey. "You didn't think I was going to find out? Well guess what? My mom died last night and her sins did not die with her."

I felt like I was in a movie that was running in slow motion. The blast that shattered the door made the wood chips fly everywhere and made everyone duck for cover. "Freeze. It is the FBI everyone put their hands up." Everyone in my family was stunned. I watched my mother's eyes become watery as the dogs ran through her house. Shit was disrespectful ripped apart and thrown everywhere. We all sat tight lipped and handcuffed to the floor. An hour later we were still waiting on the head detective. I heard a familiar voice walking through the door demanding officers to make sure they searched everything.

I turned around to see who it was. Oh my God! It was creepy Trevor, the nerd from my class. "Hey Julisa you never expected this huh? Now do you want to date me?" I spat in his face "you dirty motha fucka." "Be nice, you see I was going to let you go now I have to charge you with assaulting an officer." My father looked at me letting me know to stay quiet and not to feed into Trevor's, or whatever his name was, shit.

Trevor turned to my father, "so big man you thought you would get away again. You should have stopped five years ago. Now you are definitely fucked. Thank goodness some people don't live by the code of the streets. There are talkers… Nothing to say? I bet if I took your beautiful daughter and wife and let the officers group them in the back you might talk like a bitch." My father's eyes slanted letting Trevor know he knew better and to watch what he said or his family might end up being dead.

We were all escorted in the back of the paddy wagon and sat

silent until my father spoke. "Nobody is to say anything until my lawyer arrives. If anybody gets a call make sure that is the first person you hit up." Davi sat quiet and turned to the side not acknowledging my father. Acting like we were strangers. "Davi we will have a time to talk about everything I am sorry about your mother." Davi huffed, "yeah ok".

When we got to the holding cell, they separated us by sex so me and my mom went together and the rest went their way. I sat next to my mom and laid my head on her lap. It was too much to handle. I was so stressed I ended up falling asleep for a couple of hours I woke up to see my mother biting her nails in thought. "We are going to be ok Jul. You know that right? Your father won't let anything happen to us." I didn't know if she was convincing me or herself. "But mom he has no control of what is going on." "I believe in him. He has been my man and husband for over 30 years and now and I will not stop believing in him."

I turned around not wanting to let her know I didn't believe. I could tell it was nighttime because I could see that the streetlights just came on. "Mrs. Santana, your phone call." My mother got up and disappeared for 15 minutes. I heard her screaming "no give me another call it didn't go through". "Mrs. Santana that will be all" two police officers dragged my mother back in the cell. "Julisa the lawyer phone is disconnected" it seemed like her face had taken on years from the time she had left the cell to make her phone call. All the stress she hadn't wanted to believe was now showing on her face.

"Your turn sweatheart" a younger police looked at me and chuckled. Who was I going to call it was not part of the plan. The only one I could think about was Q. I prayed to God while I walked towards the phone hoping he would answer. Just when I was giving up hope on the third ring he picked up. "Q, it's Jul. I am at the precinct. They locked me and my family up. Can you come get me? Please?" "I am on my way." It was like a wave of relief hitting me and at that moment I knew who I wanted to be with. It was Q that I thought about when I was fucked up. He was the one that made me happy.

It took getting locked up to realize that I wanted to be his wife and that Pito was my past. I needed to let him know what happened but first I needed to get my family out of this situation. Q came and was able to bail me and my mother out we were the only ones that were not facing charges serious enough not to have bail.

"Mom this is Q, Q this is my mom." My mom unexpectedly gave him a hug and said "thank you young man". "No problem, I am sorry we had to meet this way." By the time we were let out it was day light. "Q can you please take us to the house" I gave him directions to my parent's house. When we got there the house had been pad locked and none of the cars were in the driveway. We ended up breaking the back door so my mother could grab some of her stuff. She found one of the safes that hadn't been found and pulled everything inside from Jewelry to passports.

The next stop was the attorney's office that was located in Manhattan. I was so pissed the Santana in me set in. It was now game time. Just as we pulled up I spotted the attorney with boxes rushing out of his office. "You going somewhere?" "Ms. Santana, what's up?" He looked like he was guilty of something and Q must have felt the same vibe because he pressed him. "My father is in jail and he told me to come see you." "I am no longer his attorney." "Oh yes the fuck you are." "Calm down baby girl I got this you and your moms go wait in the car." I don't know what he said but whatever it was made him start to see things our way again. Q waved us to come back.

The attorney made calls and was able to find out that Papi, David and Chulo were facing kingpin charges and a couple of counts of murder. Also that someone we knew had given them up. Everybody knew that when the feds were involved you had been under investigation for a long time, while they built their case. All of our accounts had been frozen so we didn't have access to any money except for the small amount my mother had gotten from the safe.

Q had given the attorney money to put him on a retainer which I promised to pay back and we walked out feeling a little lighter. Q offered for me and my mom to stay with him but my mom decided to go stay with her sister. Q and I hadn't spoken about nothing but my family and getting shit right but I could tell something wasn't right. He seemed distant even when I got out of jail he hadn't even given me a hug or shown no love but I had enough problems at this moment than to deal with this thing between him and Pito. He got me a rental car and instead of offering me to come home with him he blew me off and told me he had shit to do. He would see me. I wasn't going to get all emotional. My family was in a fucked up predicament and since I was a Santana I had to step up my game.

I had to find a way to get money I just kept driving around for what seemed like hours and by the time I looked up I was at my grandmothers. She had a 3 bedroom apartment in Brooklyn that she had lived in for the past 40 years. It was where my father and his 6 sisters and brothers had grown up. My cousin Miko lived with her and the other bedroom she used as a guest room. I wasn't trying to go the dorms I needed to be as close to my father as I could so I could think about what he would do.

I rang the buzzer and heard Miko voice yell "who is it"? "Julisa!" "Wow. To what do we owe the pleasure?" "Come on Miko let me in." I heard the buzzer and reached just in time to pull the door open. I rode the five floors in the pissy elevator that was known for breaking down. I don't know how Abuela (Grandmother) lived like this, but she was a stubborn old woman and never would move out no matter how much my father pleaded. Everybody thinks it's because my youngest uncle Danny who was doped out would still come for a hot meal every once in awhile. If she moved he wouldn't know where to find her.

I found the door slightly opened when I got off the elevator and proceeded to the living room. "Mi Jul! (My Jul) Como ta (How are you?)" "Bendicion Abuela (God Bless you Grandma)." "Dios te bendiga Nina (May god bless you child)." It was customary to acknowledge older folks in that manner. "Did you hear about Papi?" "Yes I did. I was waiting for you." My grandmother sat on the couch with one hand holding her rosary and the other the bible. "I have been praying for him. I knew you would come." "I don't know what to do!" "Listen you came to relax and that is what you will do! Don't worry about it, it will come to you. It is in your blood. I just cooked. Are you hungry?" Damn until she said it I hadn't even thought about the fact that I hadn't eaten in a day. "Sit down I am going to make you a plate."

I ate like it was my last meal. I don't think I have ever eaten so much. My grandmother prepared the guest room for me and I dragged my ass back there in a slow stupor. I fell asleep with all my clothes on. It's like my body needed the sleep. My dreams flashed back to when I was 10 years old and I had finally realized that my father was not your ordinary 9 to 5 father.

Saturday nights were usually girl's night in for me, Miko and Mami. My mom would have a lady come in that she knew growing up in Dominican Republic do our hair, nails and feet. We were usually not allowed to go downstairs because Papi was having his weekly investment meetings. Mami was being her usual difficult self. This was the third time that Greisy had taken off her nail polish and my mom was still unhappy. "Julisa do me a favor and go in the downstairs bathroom and grab me some acetone so Greisy can do my nails over."

"Mami send Miko!" "Julisa Santana don't let me whoop your ass go get it now." I reluctantly went down the stairs and past my father's conference room. As I walked by I heard a lot of yelling. Scared, I tried to rush by into the bathroom when I heard a loud scuffle in the room. My curiosity won over my fear so I decided to look through the crack in the sliding doors. There were at least 20 men sitting around the conference table with my father and uncle at the head of each side.

Cholo get the packages. My father's long time friend walked around and handed what looked like packages of brown sugar to everyone except one person that was sitting at the table. The guy looked around scared. P what's going on?

Cholo grabbed him by the neck with a gun to his head. "Let me get rid of him right here P." "Not in my house take him back to Brooklyn and throw him to the birds." I heard the man cry, "please P I have a son. Please. "So what? I have a family and you thought you could cut corners and make mine starve? How long did you think it would take me to figure it out?" "Please P, give me another chance.

Come on I knew about you and Carmen the whole time and I never said anything. Does that not count for nothing? Please don't do this to my son." "Don't worry about it. He will be taken care of. It's not his fault you aint shit." They dragged him out of the room, opened the door and I quickly slid in between the door and the wall. I looked up and caught my father looking right at me. After that day even though he knew I knew I never said a word and neither did he.

I woke up knowing exactly what needed to be done.

QURON JACKSON

I was feeling a way. The guilt was getting to me. I had to either come clean to Jul or put her home girl in her place so she would be too scared to even come to Jul with no bullshit. Before I could even get to it Jul had called me from the precinct and I had to end up bailing her and her mom's out. I did it because in the back of my head I knew I had feelings for this girl and she was my connects' daughter. It was a smart move for both business and personal reasons. I didn't know what she would have to say about her and her ex man but my pride wouldn't even let me ask her. After everything she was going through I knew our relationship should be the last thing on her plate.

It was fucked up that I had to meet Jul's mom under those circumstances. She was a beautiful older woman that looked exactly like Jul. Very strong, manicured and well put together older woman that smelled of money. I offered for them to stay with me but the mother opted to stay with family. I paid for Jul to get a rental. I wanted her as far as possible from me until I had my mind right. I stayed silent the whole time. I had nothing to say. The more I said, the more she would know she had broke a nigga.

Two days passed and I was starting to get worried she hadn't called or anything. I rang her number and let it ring until the voicemail came on. I hung up. Messages were not me. I headed to the block. Shit business never stopped. I was contemplating my next move how I would reup since Davi was now locked up. I had to figure out who I wanted to deal with. There were a lot of providers out here but no loyalty to the game and a lot of underhanded shit going on. So a dude had to be selective on who he fucked with. Also quality was everything I was known for my product I couldn't provide my customers with no bullshit.

I felt my cell phone vibrate and looked down to see an unknown number. Usually I wouldn't answer it but curiosity got to me. "Can you meet me somewhere?" "Everything good?" "Yeah just need a favor, how long before you can get to 42nd?" "Give me fifteen minutes." When I pulled up I spotted the rental. I waited for Jul to jump in my ride. I watched her mesmerized. She had a mean walk and even though she was dressed in jeans, boots and a hoodie she was still sexy. Her hair was in a pony tail with a Yankee fitted on.

"So what's good?" On the phone Jul had said she needed a favor and right now the way I was feeling she could have gotten whatever she wanted. "I need a piece Q." I chuckled and almost choked on the toothpick I was chewing on. "I am serious!" "For what?" "You know what forget about it, I thought you could look out damn." She grabbed the door handle and opened the door. I grabbed her shoulder "calm down, baby girl I got you. I have to handle some business then I will meet you in a couple of hours at the crib."

Even though I knew I could have given her some shit I had at the crib, I wanted to cop something she could handle. Besides that, it wouldn't hurt to have her at the house. Hmmm. I drove to the Runners spot and copped a .22 that was clean. Finished up my running around and headed to my crib. I wanted to get ready; shit, shower and shave so I could follow Jul to wherever she was headed. I wasn't trying to let her get caught up in nothing she couldn't handle alone. Even though shit was rough with us right now I was still feeling her and didn't want anything to happen to her.

By the time Jul came it was getting dark out and the cold night air made me go in change into a sweat suit. I didn't know what she was about to do so I had to prepare in case it was going to be a long night. I smelled her perfume before arrival was announced. "So where is it?" Damn she came straight for business and here I am thinking I might get some of that good good before the long night ahead. "I got you; damn you would think you never fucked wit a nigga the way you treating me." "Damn Q, I'm sorry. It's just that my mind is fucked up. I can't stand the thought of my father and Davi being in jail and all that shit is eating at me."

"Did you eat?" I decided to stay and eat. The last time I could remember eating was at my Grandmothers and it had been two days since then. My stomach felt like it was in my back. Sophia cooked a nice shrimp fettuccini with garlic bread. I even asked for seconds. After dinner we sat and watched T.V. It felt good to snuggle with Q for a moment. I dozed off for what seemed like minutes but ended up being hours. I woke up to find that it was already eleven o'clock. Q was watching the news and it took everything in me not to get up and give him some.

The only thing that kept me focused was my family. I had two spots to hit tonight and I had grabbed the piece from Q in case there were any problems. From Q's house to the Bronx was a little ride so to kill time I called my mother and checked on her and seen how she was holding up. She had spoken to my father but right now they had no news on who was talking so we were just waiting until the next step.

The spot was a 24 hour tire repair shop. When I pulled up there was a Toyota in front of me getting serviced by an older man and two big Spanish guys that looked out of place like they should be guarding a hip hop artist or something. "What you need Mami?" "I came to talk to Chino." "There is no Chino here." "My uncle Ton sent me. I am P's daughter!" The older man signaled to one of the dudes and pointed to the back. "Follow him Mamita." I followed him down a long hall past a pissy bathroom and went down some stairs. We reached a door that looked like it was made for Fort Knox and came to a stop. He grabbed the phone on the side. "Yo! We have company!" "Who the fuck is it?" "P's daughter." I heard the door unlock and slightly open. The bodyguard pushed me towards the door. "Go ahead don't be scared" he smirked and sat next to the door and watched me walk in.

I wasn't prepared for what was behind the door. There was a guy cooking work on an industrial stove and three women seated bagging product. One was nursing a baby and they were all gossiping like it was a regular Saturday at home or something. Nobody stopped to acknowledge me as I kept walking past everything to an open door.

The room was set up like an executive office of a midtown Manhattan building. There was another body guard and what looked to be a well suited teenager playing golf on one of those tees. I looked around mesmerized by the fact that right outside the door seemed like a totally different place. This was getting on my nerves, where was Chino? I was here to do business. "Come in, sit down" the young teen turned around to reveal the face of an older man that seemed like he should have been a scientist, mathematician or something. This couldn't be the same Chino that was feared in the Bronx? A stone cold killer that was running a million dollar empire. "So you are P's daughter." "Yeah, you're Chino." "That's me all 4foot 11 inches of Puerto Rican persuasion!" I laughed which turned into a cough. Embarrassed that my face had revealed what I was thinking.

"So how can I help you?" "I came to talk about business", now he laughed like I was joking. I ignored him and kept talking. "Listen my pops is not able to make moves as you may know since he is in a little predicament and all. But I came to tell you that I am able to provide the same prices and quality but now you will be dealing with me. There will be no round table until further notice. If you are interested here you go. I handed him an envelope it contained an invitation to meet with me in the Diamond Suites hotel with a room key. He grabbed the envelope and said "I will be there".

My plan was going just well. One down, many more to go. I awoke that day at my grandmother's and it came to me, I am a Santana, it is in my blood. My whole life I had been raised on drug money. It was my turn to make money. Gone were the days that I was in Fordham with Becky and Lori taking classes. I was the daughter of a Dominican Kingpin and it was my time to shine.

That day when I woke up I hit the corner store and copped a prepaid phone. My grandmother had given me my uncle Ton's number so I was ready to start making the first steps in my plan in action. "Tio (Uncle) it's me Jul." "Como ta todo? (How is everything?)" "Todo ta bien? (Everything is ok)" "But everything is going to be much better now that I am ready." "You're ready!" "Yeah I am ready." With that nothing else was said I had never called my uncle so I figured he would know the deal. He had gotten deported 5 years ago for some heavy felony charges and now he owned half of Santiago which is a city in Dominican Republic.

The weeks that followed I started receiving chocolate, flowers, teddy bears and all kinds of gifts and on each card were the name and address of everyone that was on the table. The last package I received was two round trip tickets to Dominican Republic two weeks from Saturday instructing me to bring my closest and most loyal friend. I decided not to schedule a round table meeting since I didn't know who was talking and got my girl who worked at the hotel to cop me rooms for all my guest for the Friday before I left to Dominican Republic. I had two weeks to meet with everyone and schedule to pick up the money for my flight the next day.

My next stop was the Dominican Salon to meet Jose that ran Manhattan. Everything went well except for his questions about whether or not my father knew what I was doing. I dismissed it. I was my father's daughter and when the drop was set and money in my hand, that would speak for itself. We had lawyer's fees to think about. Fuck the pride shit.

I decided since it was going so well I would make one more stop before my night was through. I was meeting Kurt at the Jamaican restaurant. It was going on 3 a.m. and the spot was still pumping. I went up to the cashier to order my food and requested to speak with Kurt. She started talking Jamaican and pointing my way. My instinct told me to bounce but money and my family kept me grounded. She told me to wait out front and somebody would be right with me.

After 20 minutes I was ready to bounce when a dred came out with a scar on his face from ear to ear. "Get in." I jumped in the passenger side of the Nissan with dark tinted windows. He started the car and I felt the point of a knife at my neck. "Don't turn around bitch, who fucking sent you?" I felt my heart drop. I didn't even think about this. I was so busy trying to make money and the other two had gone so smooth my guards had went down. I knew I couldn't reach for my piece since it was in my boot and any movement would have made him slice me.

I watched as the dred drove around the corner and tried to pay attention to where I was being taken. The fucked up part was that no one knew where I was. Just then the car was blindsided. The impact made the guy that had the knife to my neck lose control. I instinctually grabbed the door handle.

They were so busy trying to see what happened that they forgot about me. As I ran towards the restaurant I turned around to see it was Q. I headed back towards the accident. "What up man? " Q had his gun flashing, "is there a problem?" "Wah gwon?" "That is my wife you trying to dead."

"She fi know har place! Badman nuh talk money wit dem that squat to piss. Ya dun know! Unno take tings fi joke? Dis seriass business brethren" "No disrespect, she jumped the gun I'll talk to her." Jul get in the car now. "Where Kurt?" The dred grabbed his two way and said Q's name and got back in the car. Q got in the car mad, "what the fuck are you thinking Jul this is not a fucking movie. These dudes will dead you. They don't fuck with women and don't respect them." "I had everything under control and how did you know how to find me." "You didn't really think I was going to let you tote a piece without knowing you were good?" I sat back adrenaline still pumping. We sat in front of the building and waited for the go ahead to come up.

While waiting on Kurt I gave Q the run down. He agreed to help. He said he would be the money and provide the muscle. Since I was the connect we were a match made in heaven. The rest of the invitations went smooth since a lot of these men already knew Q from Davi. They also knew the product and that we were about our business.

JULISA SANTANA

As we exited the airplane, the heat of the Dominican Republic hit me exciting everything in me. I wondered why it had almost been ten years since my last visit. The Merengue band was playing their instruments as I watched the tourist stop and watch the band and some others stopped to dance. I looked over at Q and wondered if he knew how to dance Spanish music. I made a mental note for us to make a trip back when it wasn't just about business.

Not sure what to expect we continued our tip as tourist and went to baggage claim for our luggage. "Julisa Santana!" "Yes!" I turned around to see a 300lb dark chocolate monster of a man. Not sure who he was and what he wanted I turned to see where Q was. Before I could grab his attention away from the carousel, I was grabbed in a bear hug and lifted off the ground by this beast of a man. "It's your cousin Junior." Amazed and glad, I laughed. "Conyo (Damn) Junior you are not the same scrawny little dude that used to follow me and Miko around. You are fucking huge." "Yeah times have changed. So where's your stuff and your fine ass friend that I know will want to stay with big Papi." I laughed and got louder as Q walked up right on time to see what the joke was about. "Q this is my cousin Junior, Junior Q." Q put his hand out and pulled it back when he realized Junior wasn't going to shake his hand.

Junior grabbed my hand leaving Q holding the bags as we walked towards the exit. "So what's up cousin, what's new in the town?

How's the family holding up with all the shit popping of? How is Davi, Tia (Aunt) and Tio (Uncle)? What are they saying about the charges? Who is talking?"

"One thing at a time, Abuela and Miko are good. Always fighting but can't live without each other. Danny is still on that shit and the last I heard he was still with Kelly, even after she filed those attempted murder charges on him. My father and Davi are as well as expected even though they are where they at." They continued to be soldiers.

I turned around to see if Q was alright. I could see in his face he was fuming. If Junior wasn't family he would have screamed on him.

"Baby you good back there? You need my help?" "Nah I am good", I turned back around to continue my conversation with Junior. "As far as who is talking it is still under investigation. " As much as I respected the fact that Junior was family I didn't want too many people involved if they didn't need to be.

Junior opened the door to his Forest Green Rover and popped the trunk to let Q put the bags in. "I can take your friend to a hotel near the crib." "Nah. He is staying with me." Q opened the back door and slid in slamming the door as if he was slamming Junior. In the twenty minute ride my cousin put me on to how the operation was ran in DR (Dominican Republic). The whole time he spoke in Spanish so Q wouldn't understand.

According to him my uncle had been transporting product to my father through their cousin which was the east coast connect. The west coast was handled by my uncle's best friend since elementary school and being transported through my aunt's husband out of California. Junior and his twin brother were just playing muscle and running the crop spots making sure everybody did what needed to be done. He said he wasn't sure how the chain would change now that I was involved.

QURON JACKSON

We pulled up to the gate of Jul's people's house and I felt like a groupie. This man was living in an estate. On the drive up I saw all the little houses, kids barefoot running around like one of those infomercials-- but real life. This dude sat with two police officers guarding the entrance to his crib that had a drive way at least a mile long. Horses and exotic animals walked the property like a new age Scarface. This is the type of money I wanted to make while my mans were happy just copping a crib.

We got out and I grabbed our luggage. Jul's cousin was on some bullshit. That nigga was lucky we were in a foreign country or I would have snatched his wig back. The setup had me and Jul in separate rooms. I was hoping that we could have laid up together and cleared the air on all of the stuff that had been going on. Since we decided to go into business we had kept it strictly about that. We hadn't discussed any of the personal problems we were having. I was amped to make money and had fallen in a great spot to make it.

Although we were supposed to be resting, I couldn't. I was ready to take care of business. I made my phone calls to my peoples making sure business was running smoothly. I took a shower changed my clothes, put on a polo and some jeans and decided to walk around the crib and check it out. I knocked on Jul's door. She didn't answer. I walked down the steps that led to the back part of the house. I wondered how much some of the art they had were worth. The steps ended up leading me into the kitchen. I walked in on Jul's cousins and their mom having lunch. "Oh Quron, how are you? I am Erica." Jul's aunt gave me a hug and a kiss on the cheek. "Nice meeting you, are you hungry?" "No, thank you, Mam I am good." "Well make yourself at home." Jul's cousin Junior sucked his teeth. "Don't pay him any mind they have always been overprotective with Jul and Miko since they are the only girl cousins so you know how that goes." "I understand."

Jul's aunt looked like she was in her late 30's. She had reddish blond hair with a Halle Berry cut. She was light skinned with a nice ass body. I couldn't believe she had two sons my age. She was dressed in a sports tank top and tennis skirt. Exposing nice legs, flat stomach and a fat ass.

"Sweetie, Jul is in the back yard with my grandkids they absolutely adore her." "Can I go this way? I pointed to the double doors that led to a deck the size of three living rooms." She unlocked the door revealing what looked like an 8-carat yellow canary diamond with a triple tennis bracelet to match. Mrs. Lady was doing big things and I didn't blame duke, she was bad. I have dibbled and dabbled in old heads and let me be the first to let you know they were the shit. Memories, memories. I chuckled as I walked into the heat.

I looked over the patio to the backyard to see Jul playing football with 3 little boys. "Titi (Auntie) Jul throw it to me!" I watched amazed as she threw a perfect spiral. Too bad she done fucked up. She definitely could have been my wife and raise mine. I watched her finish playing with the kids and check the sports stats on my phone. Jul changed her clothes as well. She was now wearing a pair of shorts and a wife beater. Her hair was in a pony tail. Damn even sweaty and natural she looked like she could be on the cover of King Magazine.

"So what's up? How was your nap?" "I didn't take one needed to handle business." "Everything good?" "Yeah, Yeah. So when we meeting with your uncle?" "The report from Junior is no money making today we are supposed to be meeting my uncle at the club he owns to eat, chill and grab a couple of drinks. Tomorrow we conduct business and Sunday we are on our way home." "Cool what's the dress attire?" "Sexy and exclusive, can you handle that?" "I originated it!"

The spot was located near the tourist parts of the Dominican Republic. It had three floors of hip hop and r&b, Spanish and rock. Even though we were in a foreign country the setup looked like it could have been in ATL or NY. By ten o'clock there was a line that wrapped about a block long. When we got out the limo you would have thought we were attending a red carpet event. I had on my black Gucci suit with the shoes to match. Jul had on a turquoise dress that showed every curve on her body as if it were spray painted on. The slit on the sides showed her thick thighs. They escorted a group of about ten of us through the VIP section. Here I was on the strength of Jul feeling like an outsider. I stayed quiet and didn't play anybody too close. The only person to say more than two words to me was her aunt. As bad as she was my gut told me to stay as far away as possible from her.

The VIP room consisted of a variety of rooms where you could view all the happenings of the dance floor without being seen. We walked into what looked like an elegant restaurant. Already sitting at the table was an OG who was built like he did some serious time. He wore a navy pin stripped suit and talked in Spanish on his cell phone. There were two body guards on each side of him. Damn these people age well. It must be the water. Everyone took a seat at the table leaving me with the closet one to the left of him. I was already feeling a way and this I felt was a set up.

The man got off the phone and looked past me to Jul. "My favorite niece, come over here and give me a hug I haven't seen you since you were a little girl." Embarrassed Jul stood up and gave him a hug. While still holding her tightly (her back towards me) he looked at me and said, "Who are you?" "My name is Quron." "Quron what?" "Quron Jackson." "Ok!" He let go of Jul without saying another word to me and continued to catch up with Jul on the family.

The chef prepared a buffet feast of everything from lobster to stewed beef and rice. There was even a table filled with fruits and pastries for dessert. The rest of the night was cool. I showed Jul's my Spanish dancing skills and the crowd was just out to have a good time. Her uncle seemed alright. He took me and showed me the club while his son's and son in law looked at me like they were ready to pop off. All green in the face.

Jul, him and I decided to meet about business tomorrow morning in his office. He told Jul's clown ass cousins the plan and left the building early dragging his bad ass wife that wasn't trying to go with him. Still tired from the trip Jul and I left an hour later. I was fucked up drinking that Dominican Rum Brugal. Even though I wanted to be laid up with Jul my pride had me fucked up. I felt that we had too much shit to clear up. Don't get it twisted I would still fuck her. It was whether or not she could be taken seriously or not. Plus I wasn't trying to mess up my money with feelings involved.

I was up by seven even though our meeting wasn't until nine. I walked into the kitchen to find Jul's aunt in a sexy night gown bending down in the refrigerator. She was exposing a nicely trimmed plump pussy. It took me too seconds to stop looking and started coughing so she would know she wasn't alone.

She stood up with an apple in her hand looked me over and

looked at my pipe that had grown. She smirked. "Is there something I can help you with?" Embarrassed I said, "Nah, I'm good." I turned around almost running into the chef that was walking in for her breakfast rounds. I decided to go upstairs and catch up on sports center and call my people and find out how business was. I stayed in my room until it was time for breakfast. Jul and I ate outside on the patio and entertained the kids until it was time to go.

There were 6 of us in the limo ride up to Ton's office. I watched the scenery and took in the sites and tried to get a feel of the people. "Quron, you have to come when you have more time. There are a lot of places here you would really enjoy seeing." I nodded acknowledging the fact that this was a beautiful country. I definitely needed to come back. "This should be you and my nieces last time up here for business. Hopefully with all the right people we can set this thing up to work like clockwork." I looked over to see Jul's cousin festering. "Pops why you treating this nigga like he somebody, he is just Jul's boy toy." "What? Junior you need to stay in your place. I have this!" Ton turned around and faced Junior. "This boy toy makes over 10 million dollars a year for your uncle. He is about his own business; not living off who his father's reputation." Junior's mouth closed as he heard my figures. I looked away. This wasn't supposed to be about me. It was family business. I loved seeing her cousin looking stupid in the face tho. Everything in me wanted to knock that mother fucker out.

But I knew I was killing him even more because he had gotten green in the face. "Do you remember your godfather? I don't know if you were too young." "Of course pops. He took me everywhere. I loved him he was like family. But what does that have to do with this cat right here." "Your godfather is Quron's father." I turned away from the window. "You knew my father."

"Yes your father was my closest friend. My right hand. I've known your entire family since I was a kid and we lived in Brooklyn. Quron, we will talk tonight and you can ask me anything you want." I didn't know what to say. I was impatient and the anticipation about knowing about my peoples had me going stir crazy in the limo. I turned around and looked out the window again as one tear dropped down my eye. I wished I could tell my brother Jus, if he were still alive.

We rode into the parking lot of the place that housed Ton's office space. In the back there was a helicopter that fit 6 people including the pilot. We were escorted on and I was positioned to sit next to Jul's uncle. I wasn't used to not knowing where we were going and Jul didn't seem to be uncomfortable about our destination so I just rolled with it. I had never been on a helicopter so I was a little shook. It was funny how I had been shot at and almost killed many times but a helicopter had me nervous. "Q, our destination is 15 minutes away" I looked over at him grateful. He must have caught my vibe.

"Listen, I want to tell you a little about me and how I run my operation and my history with your family. I didn't want to have all ears on us so that is why I didn't elaborate before." This dude was smart the noise of the helicopter would not allow anyone else to hear our conversation at the same time not making it obvious that we were politicking.

"Currently, I have all product transported to a small city on the east coast via cruise ship. We have a couple of people on staff that make good money from our operation by living a double life. Once it is shipped to the warehouse everything is packaged like a business to the different countries and states through the airlines. We have people in our pockets everywhere and none of them know each other. If you are allowed to become part of my team I do an extensive 6 month background check on you and your family. We are more thorough than the FBI. I don't play when it comes to my money. There are only 4 people that would not die if they fucked up my money and that is my mother, my brothers and the other two are already dead. One of those people was your father. Your father and I grew up in Crown Heights, Brooklyn…"

When we landed I instinctively drove to Maw's house not even asking Jul what her plans were. In deep thought I assessed the whole weekend, my relationship with Jul and all the drama with Ali. I hadn't spoken to him since I had let him go after taking care of his little friend. As we pulled up in front of Maws building I seen a figure that looked like my moms Nicky heading towards the buzzer. I wasn't in the mood for her bullshit and her always begging for money especially in front of Jul. Don't get it twisted I wasn't ashamed of her because everybody has family problems. It just was not the time.

"Hey Maw. What up Nicky? You remember Jules, Maw right?" "Yes baby how you doing?" "Good Mam." "Jules this is Nicky my moms. They gave their hellos and I watched Nicky stare her down like she was trying to place her face. Seeing them together made me a little sick. They resembled each other more than even me and Nicky. I hadn't realized that what they say is true you end up choosing someone like your mother even if you don't want to. I watched from a far as Nicky quizzed Jules about herself, caught up with Maw and grabbed her bills that needed to be paid. Ready to head home and maybe take Jules with me.

"Maw you know what a small world Brooklyn is that Jules uncle used to hang with daddy maybe you or Nicky know him." "What is his name?" "Manny Santana", I looked over to see Maw look at Nicky and seen her face go to grey like she had just seen a ghost. "Yeah baby I know him, Maw responded." Nicky stood up and said "Maw I am going to go now". "I thought you needed that money." "No that is ok I will just see you another time." I had never known for her to give up any money but not wanting to make a scene in front of Jul I waited for her to hit the door and followed her into the hallway to find out the deal.

"What's going on who is Manny?" "Quron right now is not the time I will come see you next week it's not a big deal." I let the elevator close and decided to ask Maw when I wasn't with Jul's. With Nicky you can never find out the truth. I went back in the house to see Maw cleaning up and Jules watching TV. I pulled Maw to the side "what is going on with Nicky?"

"Listen Quron it is not my place to tell you nothing about your parents it is up to Nicky, just know this -- your friend Jules, her family is no good. You hear me? No good." I didn't want to press on. I knew Maw when she said she wasn't getting involved she wasn't. I had to find Nicky. Shit could never be smooth. There was always something going on.

A couple days passed and like clockwork, the product began flowing. I was the go-to guy in the streets. We started moving major weight. The product was so proper even those that usually didn't rock with us began copping from us. It was what it was… money was money. Jules and I came up with an arrangement where she was the middle man between me and her peoples and I ran the streets. It kept us both linked in and neither one of us completely dirty. I looked high and low to find Nicky and had even given the block word that if they seen her to call me no matter what time. Surprisingly she had been nowhere to be found.

I really wanted to see Julisa and it had been awhile since I had felt the touch of a woman. Of course I could have called one of QV (Quron's victim) but unfortunately this broad had gotten in my head. I loved that she had hustle, wasn't stressing my whereabouts and had kept it strictly business. I dialed her number and as I waited for her to answer I quickly thought of a reason to meet with her. I didn't want it to seem like I was stressing her. She answered on the 2nd ring, "What up"? "What's up?" "You busy tonight we need to talk." "Nah I am good." Alright I will be at your house around 7." "Make it 8." "Ok"… and we hung up.

JULISA SANTANA

Q picked me up at eight sharp. He seemed serious and we hadn't really seen each other since we came back from Dominican Republic. I hadn't pressed him about us. Since he was carrying it strictly business, so was I. I didn't want to seem like one of those girls that was thirsty and needed a man. Honestly I was so busy that a relationship was the last thing on my mind.

It seemed like nowadays my life consisted of school, business and relaxing. Davi and my dad had been denied bail. So me and my mom made weekly visits to give him updates. Before I could even tell him about Q and I going into business he had already heard. We kept our conversations simple since we were always under investigation. Money was looking right so I dropped the last attorney since he couldn't be trusted. I hired a new legal team. Things were looking better than the initial charges. At first everyone was facing 15 to 20 years charges and now it was looking more like 5. They had an informant that they were keeping real close. But as everyone has their price.

Pito called a couple times but I never answered the phone. He left a couple of messages that brought me to tears. It's tough when you have been with someone so long but in an instant what you thought to be true no longer is. Was it his fault that the CO was having a baby or was he just in a predicament he couldn't get out of? The problem was I moved on but I didn't know what was going with me and Q. After business was out of the way I wanted to address everything that was going on and come clean about the Pito situation. We drove in silence as we reached The Savoy. It was an upscale restaurant in Manhattan that just opened up.

We were escorted to the front of the line and seated in a dimly lit section of the restaurant that appeared to be the VIP section. I ordered a glass of wine and excused myself to take a hit before I could deal with working out any situation, business or personal. I was using a little more lately. With everything going on it seemed like my usual high wasn't getting me where I needed to be. I knew when my pops came home I could go back to recreational use.

I came back to the table to see Q speaking to a light skinned girl that looked familiar. "Jul you remember Celeste from Spring Break? This is Julisa." She gave me a half ass "hello", excused herself and kept it moving. She is lucky that Q and I didn't have a title because I would have dusted her ass rolling up on my man unannounced. Pissed, I no longer wanted to discuss anything to do with our relationship. It had just become strictly business.

Who did he think he was? I wasn't one of his victims.

QURON JACKSON

It seemed like it was never a good time for me and Jules. Out of nowhere shorty from ATL rolled up on me at Savoy. Her baby daddy was just traded to the Giants so she moved too. She was in the area and ready for a second rendezvous. I gave her the quick heave ho and tried to act like I didn't see the tension between her and Jul. I ordered an appetizer and tried to change the subject to business. It was always easier to talk about making money then dealing with our personal shit. After I quickly made up some shit to discuss about shipment and a better way to make sure everybody received shipment in time, I sat back waiting for the right time to bring up me and her.

I watched Jules and was mesmerized by her scent, she was dressed in a pair of jeans with a nice gold top. It was sheer and showed off her bra and full C cups breasts… didn't leave much to the imagination. It seemed like years since I had laid up with her and I was excited just sitting next to her. I was still pissed about the shit with her old dude and although I knew we hadn't put any titles to us, I still felt betrayed. I looked down at my black rubber band and tried to see if she still wore hers. Her hands were under the table making me feel like she was hiding them on purpose.

"Listen. I know we haven't discussed us on a personal note and I am not one to beat around the bush so I want to just come straight out with this. I know you and your ex are trying to work shit out.

I don't want to make our personal situation affect our business, you feel me?" Jules looked at me and her face dropped, "Q where did you get that from?" "Listen you know the streets talk and plus as big as NY is everyone knows everyone else." I watched Jules trying to get her thoughts together. We sat there in silence for what seemed like forever.

"Listen Q, I am not going to sit here and lie to you. I have been with my ex since you and I got together… but I like you a lot…and me and him have history… I am just confused about things. It doesn't take away from the fact that I am feeling you and taking us seriously. I am sorry that you had to hear that from someone else. From now on if I have any doubts or thoughts about us I will let you know before anyone else does."

I respected the fact that Jules kept it real but hated that she was torn between me and dude. I didn't want to make her choose. So I was going to go with the flow. As much as my pride wanted to just diss her, my heart and my manhood wanted to lay up with her even if it was just tonight.

We enjoyed the rest of the night had a good time. Without discussing it we went to my house for a nightcap. The next morning I felt rested and snuggled up to her warm body as I watched her sleep. In the back of my mind I felt like a sucka but I didn't want to let her go. I grabbed my phone to hear the faint voice of Nicky on the other line. "Listen Q I am ready to talk." "Nicky?" "Yeah I am at a rehab in Connecticut, can you make it here by 2pm today?" "Without even thinking I said "yeah", anxious and happy that just maybe Nicky was finally going to get off that shit and ready to hear what the big secret was. Happy about how life was going, I kissed Jules from head to toe let her know I was ready for round 3.

I made it to the rehab in half the time it would normally take; listening to the new Nas had me floating on the highway. I was hoping that this wasn't one of Nikky's schemes. When I arrived at the facility it was a real nice fenced community. I was wondering how Nicky could afford to pay for it. I sat in the visitor's waiting room and waited for Nicky to come down.

When she walked up on me I didn't even recognize her. She looked, healthy, glowing and gorgeous. I had never seen my moms clean of that shit so I didn't know how to react. I just stood up and gave her a hug, something I had never done before. I felt her body go limp like a weight had been taken off her and felt her tears hit my shoulder. I guided her to the seat and waited for her to get her composure before starting her story. "Listen Quron, before I begin this story I want you to understand that I am paying for all my mistakes and understand if you can't forgive me. Your dad and I were together since we were in junior high school. I had his back and he had mine. If he wasn't with me, he was with his friend Manny. We were inseparable. When we had Justice it was the best thing that happened to both us. We decided that day to never be without each other. We were a family. To make it official, your dad asked me to marry him a week later. Your daddy was always about making money so he was doing petty schemes, making a dollar here and there, but when he graduated from high school he became a full-fledged hustla. Your dad and Manny were the talk of Brooklyn. They expanded in all of New York, Maryland, VA and PA.

At this time Manny's older brother was the go-to guy. He created a table with all of the money makers around town. You name it, they supplied it. His brother and your dad were his best bread winners. It was nice. We were having the time of our lives. Your grandmother would take care of Just. We traveled. The money let us live nicely. After exploring the world we decided to settle down and maybe get out the game but then I got pregnant again and again and before we knew it there were four of you guys. It seemed like it was never the right time.

Your father was depressed about still being in the game. He didn't want this life for you and your brothers and sister. Our plan was to move out of New York and go to Florida or anywhere down south. Your father began having nightmares. Seemed like every night he would tell me that there was some reckless behavior that was going on in the table and people weren't what they said they were.

Annually the table had a block party at Prospect Park where everybody would come out and invite the whole borough. All sponsored by the heads of the game in New York. I went back to Maws house to drop you kids off and get ready for the night's events. We treated ourselves after a long day of giving back to the community.

Your dad was supposed to pick me up around 10pm just like we did every year. I was feeling myself. I just bought a red dress had on my high heels and had gotten my hair done by the Dominicans. But instead of being on time, your dad was nowhere to be found. At that time we didn't have cell phones so he had no way to let me know what was up. To my surprise Manny's brother was sitting in front of the building in a Limo. 'Nicky, I came to get you. Larry is running an errand for me so I am going to give you a ride.' My gut told me not to, but I had respect for the man that in the streets was considered your dads boss. I jumped in the car and that will forever be the one thing I regret."

Nicky paused. Her face lost its glow. She was in another place as she continued her story. "He raped me."

I sat fuming as I watched the tears rolled down my mother's face. "I never reached the party. Instead he dropped me off where he had picked me up and threatened that if I ever told anyone he would not only kill me and your dad but all you kids. I felt like I couldn't even walk after everything but I managed to open the car door and walk into Maws building.

Maw was still up reading her bible and surprised to see me back. She knew something was wrong. That night I never went anywhere and when your dad finally came Maw gave him some excuse about me not feeling well. Which didn't seem far-fetched since your dad knew I was not one to miss a party. After that I was never the same. It ruined me. I couldn't even make love to your father the same. It took a toll on our relationship. I was too scared to tell him for the fear of getting him killed or him killing someone.

The worst part was that being in a haze since the rape I hadn't even realized that I was pregnant. By the time I did, it was too late to have an abortion. When your dad and I decided to tell people that I was having another baby, it seemed like all the shit hit the fan. Somebody told him that they had seen me getting out of Peter's car and that we were having a full fledge affair. My behavior since the rape led him to question me and believe it. He never bothered to confront me and I never told him the truth. Your dad began a relationship with a lady named Shevette. He blatantly and disrespectfully paraded her all around town.

At this time your dad and I were living mostly apart than

together. I was already in my 8th month of the pregnancy. Not sure if I was pregnant by your dad or that monster, I let him do him and never complained or questioned him. I saw him one time driving past with her in the passenger seat, my seat… and I just broke down. I guess he felt like I gave up and wasn't fighting for him which made it easier to believe the rumors about the affair. On the day of the baby shower your dad decided to tell me that he was leaving me and that he was moving in with Shevette. I broke down and Quron, " Nicky was now gasping for air and tears were violently falling from her eyes. "I killed him."

Stunned, I sat there motionless as if I were in a movie. Everything was moving in slow motion. Nicky tried getting my attention, "Do you understand what I am saying?" I tried to focus knowing that it couldn't get any worse. I didn't know whether to hate her or respect everything she was telling me.

"Q, I had the baby and they took it away from me." "Who took it away from you, those people?" "What I am trying to say is ever since I saw Jules, I knew that she was your sister. I had to finally face up to my problems and get clean and make everything right."

I looked at Nicky like she was crazy, "How do you know she is my sister?!" I felt sick. Disgusted and waiting for some kind of response that would make me feel better about all that I was hearing I demanded an answer. "I just know!" I tried to make Nicky feel better and tried to make sense of everything. The woman I loved was my sister. Her father raped my mom. My mom killed my dad. It was too much to swallow.

I drove home and for the first time in a long time, I cried. I know street niggas aint supposed to let them fall. But I was that 14 year old boy that watched his brother catch his last breath in his hands. This monster that had created Jul also destroyed my family. Not only had he violated my mother but he destroyed my parent's marriage. My mother killed my pops out of anger, love and desperation. And above all I was in love with and had slept with my own sister. How different my life could have been if this monster wouldn't have wanted the one thing he shouldn't have had... a soldier's wife.

I knew that I was not in my right state of mind to make plans right now. I could die killing that man but I thought about my nephew that still had a life to live, my sister that was better than my mom's ever could be and my grandmother who deserved to let god take her life and not get caught up in gun play. This enemy knew my whole family. It was too close to home to just handle recklessly.

I called Suko and Loco. I needed to go out and let my mind blank the fuck out. We did our usual and met up at Loco's condo in Manhattan since he was the closest to the club we all would get nice before we headed out. I parked in the garage and made my way to the penthouse I knew Suko was already there because he had been blowing my phone up for the last 20 minutes.

Not really feeling in the mood to talk over the phone I hit ignore and just headed to Loco's. When I walked in Suko was sitting on the couch as always talking to his wifey and Loco was still getting dressed. It felt like we were young again. At least this never changed. My mans had never changed. Even when we started making money, we all stayed humbled dudes. We never got greedy, let bitches get in our head or lost focus that our friendship meant more than all the other shit.

"What up?" "What up?" "You gracing us with your presence your highness, shorty finally let you up for air." "Ha, Ha," I chuckled not wanting to talk about any of that I was scared I would break down before we even headed out. I knew I would eventually tell them but I needed to just get my mind right and get perspective on everything before I told all my family's dirty secrets.

Suko must of sensed it because he stayed quiet while we sat waiting for Loco, silently sipping our drinks and passing the blunt. We decided to go to a hood spot since I was dressed in Jeans and a button down. I was in a 'fuck it' type of mood and hadn't even bothered to get dressed up.

The spot was in the Bronx so I decided to ride shotgun with Suko and of course Loco drove his own shit. Pussy was always on his mind so he drove his own shit in case he had to slip out with some skuzzy. We walked in and the spot was packed. I wasn't really in the mood for too many people. I was hoping it was a slow night. I sat at the bar near the front trying to stay away from everybody and watched Loco walk to the dance floor and Suko walked to the outside deck to shoot dice.

I was regretting the decision to go out butt after starting my second bottle, I started feeling nice. The fucked up achy feeling I felt earlier was starting float away. After a couple of hours the spot became unbearable. I wobbled off my seat and leaped up to try to find Suko to take me home when I felt my back get completely wet I turned around to see a young dude.

"My bad OG," he smirked. "You're fucking bad, your fucking bad", before he knew what was happening I punched him and just kept on punching. I heard the crack of bones as I hit his ribs and watched his eye swell up but I kept going. Down on the ground I kicked him in the face. I was a monster but I couldn't stop. All that frustration I felt with Jul's pop I needed to take out on somebody.

I felt someone grab me and heard Suko's voice "Q, Q, you bugging let's get the fuck out here they already called 5-0". I followed Suko and Loco out the club and got in the car. We drove up the street and sat in silence for a couple of minutes until Loco said "what's up I have never seen you lose control like this in all the years I have known you. Let that shit off your back because next time you will kill a mother fucker and for wetting a shirt is not a good enough reason." I broke down and told them everything. They were the only brothers I had.

The next morning my head was throbbing from all the drinks that I had thrown back and I woke up embarrassed on how I had reacted. I made a mental note to check on the guy that I had put blows to and make sure that all his medical bills were taken care of and put a little something in his pocket.

I took a shower and headed to breakfast to meet Loco and Suko as we had previously planned the night before. We were coming up with a game plan and as you know three heads are better than one. I walked in to find them already there looking over the menu. "Aww its Mike Tyson" I smiled, embarrassed. "You got that." I sat down to order and felt relief taking over my body now that I knew I wasn't alone in this.

After sitting a couple hours shooting the shit we finally came up with the game plan. We all agreed that we could not touch Jul's Pop while he was locked up. After all he was a head of a multimillion dollar set up. Losing him would not be taken lightly. It had to be done by one of us since this was personal. We didn't need any loose ends after all was said and done. It needed to be me. This was too close to my heart. I wanted him to feel my wrath.

We all agreed that I needed to get rid of Jul. Suko and Loco left that for me to handle. Lastly, I had to position myself at the table somehow. Feeling much better my first stop was to meet Jul to get the plan into action.

I asked Jul to meet me at a restaurant in Manhattan. I didn't want us to even have the opportunity of getting confused. Plus being in public I knew her pride wouldn't allow her to make a scene in a public place. I watched as she walked in wearing a gold dress with black boots I felt uncomfortable being attracted to the woman that I slept with and now knowing she was my sister. It was like I was doing something wrong and I wanted to punish myself for feeling this way. I knew it was just part of a messed up circumstance.

I waited until after dinner was over to get down to business. "Listen, before I say what I brought you down here to discuss I want you to know that the reason I am being honest is because I respect you and would never intentionally do anything to hurt you." I watched Jul's eye's go from relaxed and having a good time to glossy and nervous.

"Look when we first started I was going through a breakup with my girlfriend. I really liked you and respected you. I mean I was willing to face whatever consequences your brother brought to me. What I am trying to say is that me and my ex are back together."

Her face changed from hurt to pissed. Jul swallowed before she spoke. "Cool, I respect your honesty and in no way should this affect our business relationship." That wasn't quite the reaction I was expecting. Although I knew our situation, she did not. I wanted her to fight and feel hurt, same as I did. Instead she remained cool. We managed to play it smooth through dessert, went our separate ways and made plans to meet up in a couple of days when the shipment was due to land.

JULISA SANTANA

I couldn't get out of the restaurant fast enough. As soon as I hit the door the tears started streaming down my cheek. How could he? Just when I started to believe that all men weren't the same. He was just like Pito. What was the difference? I might as well have stayed with what I knew. Here I was so thirsty, I caught a cab to the restaurant thinking that Q and I would finally get a chance to be together and we would go home together. I missed him. We had been so busy with business we hadn't even had time for us...so I thought. But this whole time he was with his ex. I felt so stupid.

I refused to let him know he had fucked me up. I was no dummy. On the business tip we still needed each other. He had the nerve to tell me he was being honest. Did that change the fact that he had just broken my heart? If he knew he wasn't over his ex why the fuck would he start something new? It was just plain selfish. I hailed a cab and heard myself say Pito's address. I needed to be held and truly loved.

I paid the cab and told him to wait 10 minutes and if I didn't come back out he could leave. Although I was crazy enough to come unannounced, I wasn't stupid enough to think that Pito may not be alone. The cab must have made a lot of noise because before I could even knock on the door Pito was opening his front door.

"Mi niña que paso (baby girl what happened)" I walked in the house not wanting to explain and finally let the tears come down completely. I never explained and I guess Pito must have felt when the time is right I would be ready to talk about it. He poured me a glass of wine and went into the bathroom to draw me a bath of water. Feeling drained and emotionally spent I finally took a look to see that Pito still had our picture up.

Pito called my name and I walked into see a nice bubble bath drawn and the lights dimly lit. Pito helped me undress and helped me step in the bath. I sat in there for hours and knew that this was exactly what I needed. Someone to take care of me. I was the head of a million dollar dynasty. That alone was a heavy burden to carry by myself. The Q and Pito triangle had drained me.

Every woman needs someone to take care of them. We need someone else to be strong every now and then. I could have stayed there all night but my wrinkled fingers and the goose bumps from the cool water told me it was time to face the world… or at least Pito. I wrapped myself in the plush bathrobe that was waiting for me and found Pito laying in the bed watching Don Francisco (Spanish version of Jay Leno/Jerry Springer).

"You good?" "Yeah I'm fine," I lay next to him and watched TV without saying another word. I dozed off. When I finally woke up I found Pito staring at me in the moonlit room rubbing my head. "I knew you would come back. We are meant for each other. Although it hurt me to know you we're with that dude I figured it was my punishment for being selfish by being in and out of jail and that shit with the CO."

I sat up. "P, I am not the same. I have grown up and have taken a lot of responsibility since my dad has been locked up." "I know I have been keeping tabs." I stayed quite not having anything else to say and after a while finally said "ok".

QURON JACKSON

The past month believe it or not I started to get to know Dyanna (African Girl) and realized that the second best brought some really good qualities you may have never acknowledged before. I respected her. I liked the way she treated me, she was very loyal and book smart.

She went out of her way to make me happy and never complained or argued about anything. You know to the average guy this may have been the jackpot but I just couldn't stand it sometimes. I would start fights to see if she would lose it but she never did. I needed someone to call me on my bullshit and fight. There was nothing better than make up sex.

We didn't have fire. We had stability. She was occupying my time. Although I felt messed up about leading her on, I felt like maybe I could learn to love her. I never let her stay more than 2 days at my house. I didn't want her to be too attached. When I was finally over Jul, I would have to let her go.

My plans as far as Jules' pops was working. I was cleaning up shop for her without her even knowing. I needed him out and did not want to bring about any suspicion by being too thirsty or too helpful. The detective that was following Jul and I since Miami was no longer a problem. We were now searching for the informant. Once that was handled, all the charges would be lowered to a misdemeanor.

I was gambling on the fact that money talks. Greed would guarantee the informant's name up with no problem. I would not relax until Jul's pops was six feet under and I could get back to the basics…getting money. Dyanna and I were going to a yearly event that was being hosted by the Who's Who of New York. It was more of a networking event for me. Dyanna was a good person to bring. She was definitely eye candy and knew how to handle herself around people with money.

JULISA SANTANA

I was feeling glamorous! Initially I was hesitant to go to the event, but my pops said that it was important to show my face in order to keep control of the streets. There had to be a face that people knew was running shit. I was wearing a Turquoise and Gold gown with gold heels to match. Pito had on a cream suit with a Turquoise tie to match. The car service waited down stairs while my make-up artist completed by look.

The entrance of the hotel was packed. Pito and I got out of the car and walked into the entrance. We were greeted by Cynthia and some guy that Pito said played for the Nets. I gave her a hug. I hadn't seen her since Q's birthday party. Just the thought made my heart sink. I excused myself and went to bathroom I needed a double hit tonight. I needed to get through this night and it was important to show face.

When I came back I bumped into this dark skin girl that looked like she could have been a model. "My fault" she turned around and with a deep foreign accent said "not a problem". "I love that dress I almost bought it." I smiled and said "thank you are working that dress yourself". It was nothing like two beautiful, confident women complimenting one another. As I walked away her man turned around…it was Q.

"Jul, Jul," he paused "what's up?" I looked back at the girl and back at Q and finally said "how you doing"? I was pissed out of all places I see him here. "Jul this is Dyanna, Dyanna this is Jul." "Yeah we just met doesn't she look great?" "Yeah yeah" he looked me up and down "she looks great". "Well it was nice seeing you both" I needed to get as far as possible away from them I felt so hurt it was easier when I could picture his girl to be some ugly ass broad not gorgeous and nice.

I don't know why I didn't think about it before. Of course he would have been there. It was a Who's Who of New York and Q was that dude. This was not going to be a good night. I had to keep Pito away from Q and vice versa. Before I could try to avoid the drama Pito walked up, "Mi Nina (Baby Girl) is there a problem"? "Nah baby, why what's up?" "That dude said something to you?" "No Papi, we moved on I am with you."

 Although Pito was pissed, he knew making a scene would only make him look like we weren't good. So he played cool, but played me close the entire night. The coke was wearing off and I am sure my nerves being on edge made it go through my system quicker. I texted Cynthia to come get me away from Pito so I could go do me. Cynthia walked up. "Hey yah, damn yah so in love that yah can't chill without each other." "I turned come on girl you know it aint like that me and my baby just can't get enough of each other." Pito smiled I could tell he was eating it up.

"Is it alright for Jul to walk me to the bathroom?" Embarrassed Pito said, "Come on Cynthia, Jul is a grown ass woman."

"I will be back baby. Let me go walk this nut case," I laughed. Before he could hesitate or give me the eye I was heading to the bathroom Cynthia trailing behind me. "What is going on girl… why is he bugging… damn I knew it was serious when you texted me to give you a breather." I laughed, "Girl you know Q"? "Q, who? "Cynthia the dude in the grey suit, remember from the party" she looked over to see Q standing with the model chick. "Oh him girl the best thing you could have done is not fuck with him. Although he has a big dick he aint shit." "Bitch what you mean he got a big dick." "Girl it aint that serious me and my home girl seen him one night that is all."

"What the fuck you mean you seen him," without thinking I slapped the shit out of Cynthia. Instantly we started fighting. I felt someone pull me off her and heard my name. I turned around to see that Q had grabbed me. I heard Cynthia screaming at the top of her lungs "Pito come get your bitch before I shoot her. She over here fighting over a nigga that aint hers".

I looked at Q embarrassed "You are one dirty dude. You knew she was my friend". I watched as his girl looked confused. Pito stormed over, "What the fuck?" he grabbed my arm and yanked the fuck out of it. We got in the car and he didn't say a word to me I had never seen him so mad. I didn't know how to explain it. What could I say? I was wrong? I finally would have to admit that I still loved Q but I couldn't. I just cried in the corner of the limo and was hurt that the man that I loved was loving someone else and I was hurting Pito in the process.

QURON JACKSON

This was getting crazy I don't know what that stupid friend of Jul's said to her but she was fighting over me. I felt bad that Dyanna was placed in that predicament. Crazy thing is she was pissed for the first time! Some little clown Spanish dude came and grabbed Jul up after I stopped the fight. I was going to say something but I had a feeling that it was her ex. I guess shorty wasn't joking when she said it was all good. She ran right back to her ex.

Cynthia was probably right, Jul was juggling the both of us. Dyanna was more pissed than I thought because she asked the driver to take her home. I didn't say a word. It wasn't my fault that they were fighting. I had in no way disrespected her. She was giving herself too much importance.

The next morning I woke up to a call from the attorney handling Jul's pop's case saying that he needed to meet Jul and I in his office. I grabbed a pair of jogging pants. I wasn't in the mood to dress up after the nonsense that happened yesterday. When I walked in Jul was already waiting. I acknowledged her and sat down next to her.

"Look Jul", but before I could tell her how I felt she stopped me and said, "Listen that fight was not over you it was over the fact that she was disrespectful as my friend. I don't have any expectations from you. After all, you never seem to surprise me."

"What are you talking about?" But before she could respond the attorney's assistant called our names and lead us to the conference room.

I know shorty didn't tell Jul that I fucked her. Believe me I thought about it but a nigga had principles. Plus I knew that girl was a thirst bucket. She just wanted to fuck a nigga to say she did. But once I got to the hotel my conscious got the best of me and I went my ass home. I needed to tell Jul. I don't know why. Its not like it really mattered but I shouldn't have lied to her about Dyanna. I didn't want her to think I was a fucked up person. What was I thinking? Who gives a fuck? She is my damn sister.

Instead of revealing the real deal I stayed quiet and waited for the attorney to come explain how the case was going.

"We found out who is talking, his name is Carlos Ortiz?" I sat back. The name was not familiar. I looked at Jul to see if she knew who it was; she said nothing or gave no expression of recognizing who it was. I spoke up since it didn't seem like she was going to add anything to the conversation. "So how much time before we go to trial" "2 months." "Worst case scenario if he makes it to the stand how much time are they facing?" "5 years." "Ok."

We walked out of the attorneys office and didn't say a word to each other. Jul seemed to be in her own thoughts and I was trying to figure out how I could handle this last obstacle. She walked to her car without even saying goodbye to me. I wasn't stressing her. I didn't know what her deal was but I wasn't kissing no broad's ass, no matter how I felt.

JULISA SANTANA

I felt the sweat on my face as I walked in the private room of The New Millennium. The anticipation of what I needed to do was overwhelming. There were no other options. This dude was trying to fuck my family. He left me no choice. As I walked in the room his eyes went from scared to calm as the bullets entered his head. I looked down at his still body and spit on what was left of his missing face. It was just that quick.

Yeah I knew Carlos Ortiz. I couldn't believe it when the attorney said his name. He was a young general in my father's army that had been positioned to guard me and my moms. He had practically helped my mom raise me while my dad was fucking everybody. The same mother fucker that had introduced me to coke so that I could get rid of all the demons.

If you couldn't trust someone that had been in your life as long as you could remember, who the fuck could you trust? This year I had went from a college student trying to live a normal life to a full time drug dealer and killer. The sins of my father fell on me. I was falling in his footsteps.

I was Jules Santana. Killing Carlos made it real. I accepted my fate. This was my life. It wouldn't change when my father came home. I had gone too far and seen too many things. I grabbed my bag from the bathroom vent took off the wig, lit the match and walked to sit next to my college roommates.

I got up to dance when the fire alarm went off "Jul we have to get out of here" I heard Samantha say. "Huh!" "There is a fire, I looked around to see the whole place going crazy to get out and let her grab my arm and lead me outside.

QURON JACKSON

I gave the word to my enforcer that I wanted the snitch to disappear. He came back the next day and stated that there was no charge since it was taken care of by a chick with a nice body and red hair. I thought about Jules but she wasn't built that way. I figured she contracted someone she knew. Well it was easier for me since it didn't cost me a dime and now with a weak case Jul's pop and David were set to be released next week. I came up with a plan to follow Jul's pops. In the next two weeks, I'd see his schedule so that I could catch him at his most vulnerable state.

I hadn't really been focused on too much business since everything was running smooth. I hadn't called Dyanna. It was what it was. I had been playing low key lately, was trying to get low so when everything was said and done I would slip out of New York for good. I already made the proper plans and even invited Qahira and my nephew to come with me once everything was set.

I knew it would be a better opportunity for him and with his ball skills he could get a scholarship to any college he wanted. Maw already said she wasn't going anywhere and I figured she wouldn't. Now that Nicky was clean they were both making up for lost time. It was time for Nicky to take care of Maw.

After watching Jul's pop I found that he was having an affair with an older lady in Queens and that when he visited her he would never bring his security detail. The lady looked familiar but I couldn't pinpoint where I knew her from. I picked a weekday to handle my business since most people were at work it would be easier to sneak in and out. The lady had a nice little house everything taken care of and it looked like she had been a kept woman for a long time. I snuck in through the side door since it was the only door with a glass window.

It was a really easy break in since she didn't have any pets or a security system. I waited for her to get home from work and once I heard her car slipped on my mask and surprised her before she could make a scene. I tied her up and put her in the bedroom I didn't want to hurt her after all the only thing she had done wrong was fall for the wrong clown and I didn't want to spill innocent blood if I didn't have to.

Jules dad let himself in with his own key so when he came in he almost caught me off guard. Thankfully, he started yelling "Cathy, Cathy where are you?" I watched the older lady squirm trying to get free and placed the gun to her head to let her know I was still in the room and to quiet down. She quickly stopped moving and laid limp.

Jul's pop opened the door. "Cathy! Who did this to you?!" He ran to the bed and before he knew it I gun butted him and he fell to the floor. By the time he woke up he was chained to a chair in the basement and I was waiting for him to wake up. I hadn't gagged him, I hadn't blind folded I wanted my face to be the last one he seen before he died.

"What is this about?" "I think you know what this is about?" "No I don't!" It was pissing me off that he was denying everything. "You raped my mother! Ruined my family...and you sat there and allowed Jul and I to sleep together even though we were brother and sister. Do you not have any morals?!" I watched him contemplating what he was going to say.

"First of all, I know that it doesn't matter what I say but I will tell you everything because you deserve the truth. I never raped your mom we had an on and off again relationship, and Jul's is not your sister." What I sat down, I couldn't take all these lies and who to believe. "Me and your mom have two children together your brother Ali and Miko." "Huh!"

"Yeah we started seeing each other while she was still with your father. Our relationship became real serious when your dad started seeing another lady and fell in love with her. Your mom became pregnant with my second child and it was during the same time your father died. She was already using that shit but after that she was on it heavy pregnant and all.

So when she finally had the child the hospital called CPS (Child Protective Services) to come and take the baby because of all the drugs she had in her system. I stepped in and paid the lady off and gave her to my mom's to live with it. I have raised her as my niece and have done everything I could. And I didn't take your brother Ali because I didn't know that he was mine until your pops funeral the day I seen him I knew.

But it was the wrong place and the wrong time and it was already too late to make him mine. Julisa's mom wouldn't be able to stomach two children with the same women.

But believe me I sent your grandmother money for all you children and I loved your mom and believe it or not loved your dad as well."

I heard noises from upstairs, aww shit the lady got out. I saw Jul's pop's face change from fear to recognizing he might be saved. He tried to keep talking. "Listen, no matter what you still are going

140

to die."

I aimed the gun at his head. I heard footsteps running down the stairs. I put on my mask. Dodging bullets from his security I shot at Jul's pop and didn't stop shooting until I saw blood dripping from the side of his head and his body go limp. I managed to slip out through the same side exit.

I wasn't crazy there was no way that I was fighting an army, I wasn't superman. I ran to my car happy and excited at the same time. I finally got rid of the dirt that had been haunting my family for a long time. Jul's was not my sister. I couldn't wait to call her. I must admit it I loved this woman and I wanted to be her.

I was not allowing anyone to get in the way. We had gone through too much together and somehow every obstacle had finally disappeared. I missed her body, touch and the way she inspired me. But there was so many unanswered things like who was Miko and did she deserve to know the truth? I didn't want to say too much since all this would come back pointing to me if the right person investigated.

Maybe I would give it a day and let Jul call me about her pop's murder. Then I would come through like her knight in shining armor.

A couple days passed and no Jul. I didn't hear a word. I finally decided to call her. Damn! I didn't count on not hearing from her. "Hey Ma, what's up I hadn't heard from you in a little while what's good." "Hey Q' I heard her sniffle, "what's wrong?" My dad got shot and is in the ICU. My heart dropped. Fuck. I just figured he was dead. Who else would be able to survive a shot to the head?

I managed to say "I am sorry to hear that". "The worst part is he was having an affair with my mother's sister. Since he was shot at her place, my mother is being investigated." "Damn Baby girl, where you at? I am on my way." Scared to ask if her dad had given my name. I knew better because right now I wouldn't be breathing.

When I arrived at the hospital security was tight in the waiting area. I saw Davi away from everyone. I said my hellos and sat next to him. I didn't want to make a scene approaching Jul's right away and didn't see her so I figured I would get the info from Davi.

"What up?" "What up?" I started to say something and sensed that he was irritated so I laid back and waited for him to talk. After what seemed like hours he finally spoke "I hope that mother fucker dies," I looked at him was this a test I refused to talk I felt like I was being set up. "What's going on?"

He looked straight ahead and I seen a tear drop from his eye "that bastard raped my mother and he is my real pops. This whole time

142

I am thinking what a good guy he was to take me under his wing and he ruined my moms and killed the man that was raising me as his own." I was feeling a way. This story sounded too familiar. Were they trying to get my reaction to see if I found out? Was it a set me up?

I sat perfectly quiet "come outside with me for a smoke". Davi knew I didn't smoke but I figured if they were trying to take me out I would at least be able to run. I followed, watching all my surroundings and when we hit the front doors I eyed the paths I could take if they started shooting. But instead Davi started talking, and when he was done the tears in his eyes told me this wasn't a set up. He was a victim of an evil man that ruined many lives including my own.

Although Jul's Pop wasn't dead, he was in a coma so I was off the hook for now. I walked back in to find Jul's walking toward the exit. "Hey!" "Hey," her eyes were beet red and it looked like she hadn't slept in days. "Let me talk to you for a moment." "I am on my way home. I caught a cab, do you mind giving me a ride we can talk on the way?" "Nah, but why don't we just head to my house since its only 15 minutes away and we can have a warm meal waiting." She simply nodded her head in agreement. At this point she had no strength to argue.

I had so much to say to Jul but it was like my words were jumbled. I sat quiet during the whole trip and didn't say anything. What should I say? I thought she was my sister? Tell her that her father was a monster? That I loved her? I watched her stare out the window on our ride to my house. I felt sorry for her. She didn't seem the same from the day I first met her –enjoying a carefree life Miami.

She looked rough and tired, like life had finally caught up with her. She had the world on her shoulders. Before we got to my house, I asked my housekeeper to prepare Jul's a nice homemade soup. When we got there I took Jul's jacket off and escorted her to the dining room. I saw a slight smile on her face.

"Q, I truly appreciate this. I don't know when was the last time I ate." "You know I got you," we sat down and stared at each other for a couple minutes. "Listen I want to tell you that I made a mistake and I truly miss you. I have never been in love with any woman in my life and it scared me so I lied to you and told you that me and Shorty were serious. Fuck I had even tried to get over you but I couldn't."

I walked towards her and grabbed her hand "I want to be with you. I want you to be my lady and possibly my wife. I never stopped wearing the rubber band. It reminded me that you were somewhere in this world, even if it wasn't with me." She didn't say a word at first. Then she looked me in my eyes, "Q I love you too but you slept with Cynthia and Pito and I have been trying to work things out". "I never slept with her. Believe me she attempted to but I didn't want to ruin anything that could have been with us." "You may be trying to work out things with that dude but I know that it's not the same and that you feel the same way I do about us."

The tears started to drop from her eyes "I do love you but right now is not the time. My dad is doing bad and my family will never be the same." "Davi and my dad are beefing and my mom is being investigated." "That is why I am here to help you since we have gotten together I have always had your back and made everything right for you. Am I wrong?" She nodded, "and you have made me strive for the normal life I never even knew I wanted".

I grabbed her and stood her up from the chair and kissed her lips. "I love you Girl, you hear me." She grabbed my waist and we kissed each other like it was the first time.

I slept real good that night knowing that Jules was sleeping next to me I watched her as she slept and smelled her hair what was a combination of vanilla and coconut. I was giddy as a child I loved this woman and would do anything to be with her. I fell back to sleep and woke up to find that Jul had already gotten up. It was pitch black in my room because of the dark curtains.

I wasn't a morning person. After all, my business was done mostly at night. I heard a loud sound of glass breaking downstairs. I jumped out the bed grabbed my gun and pants and headed to see what was going on. I ran down the stairs and saw my housekeeper with two shots to the head lying next to the front door.

I walked into the living room to find Jules body spread out on the broken coffee table with two shots to the back. I grabbed her body and cradled it like I had done Just's body so long ago. The two people I loved the most could not die the same way. I heard the sound of a car screeching away and looked up at the blood stained wall that said PAYBACK MOTHERFUCKER!!

ABOUT THE AUTHOR

This is Maya Keith's first book she started writing Love, Sex and The Hustle after life experiences motivated her to put things on paper. A native from New York and currently residing in Maryland she has worked in Corporate America for 20 years. Maya has a Bachelors in Business and is currently working on a Masters in Finance. She is the mother of two children and dedicated to giving back to her community. This project was something that she started as a hobby and it ended up taken a mind of its own. Her characters are built from the people she has met, imagination and the lives that have touched hers. She hopes you enjoy her passion!

www.ingramcontent.com/pod-product-compliance
Lightning Source LLC
Chambersburg PA
CBHW071303130626
46556CB00003B/1449